Licorice Wishes

A Cherry Blossom Grove Novel

My mother has always been my biggest fan. Whether I'm writing romance,
zombies, or murder mysteries—she's proudly telling the world all about it.
From an early age, she instilled a confidence in me that made me believe I could do anything
I wanted in this life... and I have. I'm living my dream of being an author.

I'm so grateful for you, Mom.
And, since you love my storytelling but not necessarily the spice, this sweet romance series is dedicated to you.
Love you, always.

Chapter One

Glass cases of color surround me. Rainbow hues ripple around the room, touching everything from the chocolate candies to the licorice sticks and gummy worms. I grew up here, in this enchanted place full of processed sugar and happiness. Now, looking around the candy shop, all I feel is emptiness.

I tap the lollipop-shaped pen against the counter in an anxiety-laden cadence. "I can't do this," I say out loud as I nervously watch the door.

Any minute now, a representative from the nursing home in the next town over is going to walk through the front door of the shop, expecting me to sign my nana, my sweetie over to them. I thought it was best for her, but the pain deep within my soul tells me it's not.

"I'm not doing it," I say again, my voice shaking as tears fill my eyes. "I can't."

Soft fur nudges my arm, and a rumbling purr fills the space. Our cat, Pumpkin, all twenty-five pounds of him, rubs against my arm in agreement. I set the pen down and lug the orange puff ball into my arms. Burying my face into his fur, I allow a few errant tears to escape, releasing months of stress that this agonizing decision has caused.

Pumpkin continues to purr, which is rare for him. The fact he spends his days in a candy shop has done little for his temperament, and truth be told, he's usually a bit of a jerk. His purrs and content demeanor tell me all I need to know. Listening to my gut is the right decision. My nana, who is affectionately known as Sweetie by the entire town, always told me to listen to my gut. Trying to do the right thing, I ignored it. Now that the day has come to sign the papers, I can't ignore it any longer.

"Thank you," I whisper into Pumpkin's fur before setting him down on the counter. He stretches across the glass case and closes his eyes for a leisurely nap.

Looking at him now, I realize it's probably a little odd that a cat has free rein in a store that sells food. To be honest, I'm not sure it's all that sanitary. Yet...I've never questioned it before, nor have any customers. Everyone's face lights up when they enter Sweet as Pie and see our grumpy fat cat. He's somewhat of a store mascot.

Life in our small town is an otherworldly experience from most places, I'd imagine. Cherry Blossom Grove is a city in Northern Michigan that's exactly like one would expect of a town with that name. Antique brick storefronts, that have been here since the town was established in 1900, line the downtown. There are exactly three traffic lights, two bars, five family-owned restaurants, and a collection of random stores that sell everything from books to cowboy boots to plush unicorns to candy.

My best friend Abby's family runs the cherry farm just outside of town, which is big business for the area, bringing in lots of summer tourists. My grandparents fell in love with this place one summer sixty years ago when they came to pick cherries. They loved it so much that they moved here and opened their own store, *Sweet as Pie*, an old-fashioned candy shop. I'm not entirely sure why my grandpa insisted on the name, given the fact that we don't sell pies, but he found it hilarious. He would always get a kick out of tourists coming in expecting to leave with a cherry pie but leaving with five pounds of gummy bears instead. I think the name came from the nickname he gave my grandmother, Sweetie Pie, which was later shortened to Sweetie.

My parents died in a car crash when I was a toddler, leaving me with only a few fleeting memories of them. My maternal grandparents raised me. My childhood was great, magical even. Living in the apartment above a candy shop definitely has its perks. My grandpa was a fun man and always made our life an adventure. He passed away six years ago when I was nineteen. Since then, it's been just me and my Sweetie.

A little over a year ago, I noticed Nana starting to forget things more than usual, and it's progressed since then. She doesn't remember her life more often than not lately. I was concerned about her safety being alone in the apartment when I'm down in the store, so I hired a sitter to keep her company. The store keeps me so busy that I feel like she's always with a stranger, so I began to question if it was the right thing. I reached out to the closest nursing home, and they persuaded me they could give her a better quality of life.

In my heart of hearts, though, I don't think she'd want that. She's lived in the apartment above the candy shop for most of her life, so I know she wouldn't want to leave it. I'll just have to figure something else out.

The bell above the door chimes, and my pulse races as I look toward the entrance. I release an exhale when I see that it's only Ben, my friend and one of the local firefighters.

"Hey, you," I greet him.

"Hey, Evie." He smiles wide and scans the walls. "The crew is having a potluck tonight, and I'm supposed to bring a dessert."

"You sure you shouldn't try the bakery?" I tease.

"Nope. What I need is right...here." He stops in front of the toffee candy bar bits. Grabbing a white paper bag from the stack beside the candy display, he opens the front of the candy case and scoops some chocolate pieces into the bag.

"Are you sure broken bits of unwrapped chocolate and toffee are the way to go for a potluck?" I chuckle.

He looks at me with a tilt of his lip. "Nah, this bag is for me. You know I'm obsessed with this stuff. I'll grab an assortment of the wrapped mini candy bars for the guys."

"You want me to package some up for you?" I ask.

"Yeah, that'd be great."

As I bag up some treats for Ben's firefighter buddies, the bell above the door sounds again. I freeze and look toward the sound, only to see my best friend, Abby, and her boyfriend, Matt, entering.

She and Matt greet Ben. Abby wraps her arms around him in a hug. Abby and Matt used to be best friends with Ben's brother Beckett before he left town suddenly at the end of our senior year. I always thought Abby and Beckett would marry someday, but things change. One constant here in Cherry Blossom Grove is that everyone knows everyone, and we're all connected.

Matt stays beside Ben and the two chat.

Abby walks toward me and grabs my arm. "Did she come?" she asks softly.

I shake my head. "Not yet. She's late. But I've changed my mind."

"You did?"

I nod. "I can't do it, Abby. It just doesn't feel right."

Tears come to my eyes again, just thinking about sending my nana to live somewhere else.

"Oh, Evie." Abby pulls me into a hug. "It's a big decision, and you have to follow your heart. If it doesn't feel right, then it's not right. You love your nana more than anyone, and whatever you decide to do is the right thing. You'll make it work."

Abby drops her arms and steps back.

"She's still there sometimes, and I fear that if I put her in unfamiliar surroundings, then she'll be lost completely. You know? I don't think she'd want to leave her home or me."

"Yeah, totally. Makes sense. What about hiring a nurse to help you?" Abby asks.

"I've been thinking about that, and I think that's the next step. Then she can remain in her home with me and Pumpkin but still receive proper care."

Abby nods. "That sounds good. And maybe hire someone else to help you with the shop. You work too much."

"I know." I sigh. "Adulting sucks."

"Sometimes it does." Abby grins. "Please say you're going to Hazel's bonfire tonight."

"I can't. I have to stay home with my nana."

Abby whips out her phone and starts typing rapidly against the screen. "No way. You know Hazel's Memorial Day weekend bonfire is huge. Plus, it's my last hurrah before I'm drowning in cherries for the summer." She laughs.

She's right. Cherry season isn't long, but it's intense. Abby's pretty much MIA June through August as she helps her father on the farm.

Her phone buzzes. "It's settled. My pa will be at your house at nine to hang out with Ms. Sweetie. You be ready for some fun tonight."

"Okay, perfect. Thanks." I squeeze Abby's hand.

"Anytime. Hazel's bonfire wouldn't be the same without you."

The bell above the door chimes, and this time, it's the representative from the nursing home.

I pull in a breath. "I better check Ben out so I can talk with her."

"You got this." Abby shoots me a reassuring smile.

"Thanks. I'll see you tonight."

Chapter Two

I hand Nana a cup of herbal tea. "Here you go, Sweetie."

"Thank you, Evelyn, dear. Can you tell your father that the *Golden Girls* is on? You know he loves this show. Blanche and Rose make him laugh." She chuckles to herself and holds the mug of warm liquid in her hands. Pumpkin lies across her lap.

Most days, she thinks I'm my mother, and it's okay. I'm grateful she thinks I'm someone she knows. I dread the day she feels alone or scared. I know I may not be able to keep her here forever, but I'm glad she's here now. Dementia is so heartbreaking.

The representative from the nursing home was kind and understanding today when I told her I just wasn't ready to commit. I'm sure she's heard it before.

"Sure thing. I'll tell him. I wanted to let you know

that I'm going out tonight, but Abby's dad, William, is going to be here any minute to hang out with you."

"Oh, well, that's just fine, dear."

I leave Nana in the living room and load the few dishes from the sink into the dishwasher. With my hands splayed against the kitchen counter, I close my eyes and breathe deeply. Bone-deep exhaustion weighs on me. The last thing I want to do is to go out tonight, but I know my soul needs it. An evening with my people will rejuvenate me, despite how desperately my body wants to fall into my king-sized pillow top mattress at the moment.

I feel like I'm twenty-five going on sixty. Every muscle in my body physically hurts. I'm down in the shop before it opens and work until well after it closes, seven days a week. All the life-changing decisions I need to make regarding Sweetie have my brain working on overdrive. My heart is heavy, knowing I can't stop her mind from deteriorating. I'm surrounded by people who love me, yet I've never felt more alone. I wasn't always such a downer. I used to be the carefree life of the party. I mourn that life.

A shrill meow comes from below, and Pumpkin rubs against my leg, indicating he'd like a can of wet food.

"You've already had your wet food today. Go eat some of the dry stuff. It has the bits of salmon in it that you like," I reason with my cat.

He meows again, and this time, it's louder and urgent. It's a warning. He knows I'll give in. I always do.

His chubbiness is proof of my weakness. In my defense, he's no ordinary cat. He's smart and vindictive. If I don't yield to his requests, he's going to pee in my sock drawer or knock the sugar container off the counter while I'm gone. His punishments can get quite creative.

Another shriek comes from my furry roommate below. "Fine," I relent and grab a can of food from the pantry.

I scoop the vile meat concoction out of the can and onto a serving dish the way Pumpkin likes it and set his plate on the ground. "You're so spoiled." I run my hand along his back and up his tail. He grumbles, indicating he'd like to eat in peace. "Fine. I'll leave you to your food. Just make sure to keep Sweetie company tonight. Okay?"

A knock sounds, and I open the door. "Hi, William."

Abby's father pulls me into a hug. "Hey there, Evie."

"Thank you so much for doing this."

"My pleasure!" He grins as he makes his way into the living room. "Miss Sweetie. How's my girl?" he greets Nana in the jovial way he always does.

"Oh, you." Nana swats him away with a smile. She seems to recognize him, or maybe I just want to believe she does.

"She'll head to bed after *Golden Girls*," I tell William. "If you need anything, call me. The remote is beside her on the end table. There's a *Harry Potter* marathon on all weekend on channel fifty-six."

His eyes light up. "Well, Evie girl, you stay out as

late as you want. It looks like I have a date with some wizards tonight."

"I thought you'd like that." I smile.

William has loved the *Harry Potter* series since he read the books to Abby when she was young. His spouse doesn't share William's passion with the wizarding world.

"It will be so nice not having my better half yapping in my ear as I'm watching," he kids.

"I bet." I chuckle. "Okay, well. Remember, call me if you need anything or have any questions."

William places his hands on my shoulders. "We're good. Don't worry. Go have some fun."

I nod. "All right."

* * *

The drive out of town toward Hazel's land is therapeutic. I've driven out this way more than I can count, and each time led to happiness. Memories of my time on these two farms or in the candy shop in town with Hazel and Abby hold a sacred place on the highlight reel of my life. Our childhoods were pretty great.

I pass Abby's cherry farm first. It's almost cherry season, which will bring an influx of tourists to our town. The store and restaurant owners love cherry season. The quaint ambiance of Cherry Blossom Grove is a big draw with tourists. To me, it's just—normal life. In truth, I haven't traveled much. In fact, I've never left Michigan.

With the store, traveling was never really discussed. My grandparents were always working, and I always had more than enough adventure here. Summers are filled with cherries, backyard parties, and people from all over. Winters are for sledding, skiing, and cozying up in front of a warm fire.

Hazel's land is just past Abby's. Where one is rolling acres of cherry trees, the next is the same but with rows of grapes. Having a best friend whose family owned a vineyard also had its perks growing up.

I pull into Hazel's drive, which is flanked by two old willow trees. I've always loved these trees. There's something magical and grand about them. Many hours in my life have been spent swinging from their branches with my besties. Living in the apartment above the candy store, I don't have even a patch of grass to call a yard. Yet my best friends live on two of the most beautiful properties around and I got to grow up here, too.

I follow the drive past the large farmhouse and barns and out toward the grassy field where a blazing bonfire awaits. Bales of hay form a circular seating area around the flames. I park next to the other dozen vehicles that are already here and get out.

The second my car door closes, I'm the center of a group hug. Hazel, Abby, and Matty wrap me in their arms.

"Evie!" Hazel says. "I'm so happy to see you. I've missed you so much."

"I haven't gone anywhere." I laugh.

"I know, but you've been busy. It'll be great to catch up." She takes my hand in hers, and I follow her toward a table of snacks and drinks. "Plus, I have a surprise."

"What's that?"

"Remember how my parents were working on a cherry wine with Abby's parents?" she says.

"Yeah."

"Well, the cherry wine is finally ready, and it's so good." She picks up a bottle of wine from the table and pours a good amount into a red Solo cup before handing it to me.

"It really is amazing," Abby agrees.

Hazel hands plastic cups full of wine to Abby and Matt before putting her own cup between us. "Cheers to a great night full of friends and fun."

"Cheers to that," I agree and tap my cup against their cups.

We take a sip. "Yum. That's incredible."

"Right?" Abby agrees. "Our new favorite, for sure."

"And how classy are we?" I hold up my red Solo cup and wiggle it back and forth.

"Only the best wine glasses for my people." Hazel grins.

After the equivalent of at least an entire bottle of wine later, I've laughed and caught up with everyone at the party. It's so great to hang out with people my age and not worry, for once. I've become this ball of stress as of late, and I don't like that version of myself.

My back against a bale of straw, I stare into the

dancing flames of the fire. I think of my grandpa, my Pops, George Emberton, and his bright orange hair. If you asked anyone in the town to name a characteristic about my Pops, they would mention his hair color, his smile, and the life he brought into every room he entered.

I've always been proud of my red hair and green eyes both of which I inherited from my grandfather. Though, where my hair is a deeper red, his was definitely orange. I'm certain Nana and I took in the little stray cat the summer after his death because the kitten's fur reminded us of the person we so desperately missed. Unlike Pumpkin, though, Pops was never grumpy. In fact, I don't think I've ever met such a cheerful person in my life. Surely, he and Nana had to have experienced stress throughout the years, yet...I don't remember him ever worried about anything. He was always smiling, laughing, joking, and pulling pranks on the love of his life. Nana pretended to hate his pranks, but her face always carried a smile as she chastised him and swatted him away. My pops would have hated me like this—always stressed.

"Hey." Matt's deep voice pulls me from my thoughts. He holds up a wine bottle. "I've got a refill for your thoughts."

"I've moved on to water, but thanks." I smile.

He sits beside me. "Okay, no drink, but I'd still like to know what you're so deep in thought about."

"Oh, Matty." I sigh. "I don't know what to do with

my life. I decided today to keep Sweetie with me and hire a nurse, but I still feel heavy. I thought that decision would lighten my load, you know?"

"Well, what else is bothering you? The store?"

"Yeah, maybe, I guess. This past year has flown by, and all I've done is worked. I love working, but I never envisioned myself working there forever. Is that even what I want?"

"You tell me. What is it that you wanted to do before you took over the store? You had dreams. What were they?" he asks.

I chew on my bottom lip and pull in a breath. Life before—all of this—seems like it was forever ago. Scanning the area, I take in the faces of these people I've known my entire life. Some are serious in conversation. Some carry wide smiles as they laugh. Others have squinted eyes, a sign that they probably should stop drinking. The light from the fire flickers across their skin creating patches of shadows, and I see it, snapshots, of this moment.

I've always known what I wanted to do with my life. As of late, I've simply been too scared to admit it. "I wanted to be a photographer," I answer.

He slaps his leg with his palm. "Oh my gosh, that's right! We took that photography class elective together during freshman year, and you became obsessed. I remember. You always had a camera with you throughout high school."

I nod with a grin. "Yep, that was when it started."

"Ugh, I hated that class. Remember how the teacher went on and on about angles and shadows and blah, blah, blah. But you loved it."

"I did, and I'm pretty sure she never used the terms blah, blah, blah." I chuckle. Mrs. Owens, our photography teacher, changed my life. She fostered a love in me I didn't know existed prior. She taught me to see the world in pictures.

Matt bumps his knee against mine. "Well, then do that! Be a photographer. Sell the store. I bet there are tons of tourists who would love a family photo in the orchards or vineyards. Also, all the weddings performed here need a photographer. You could do really well."

"Yeah, that's true. There really isn't a local photographer. They all come in from elsewhere."

"Exactly," he agrees. "It's perfect. You'd do great."

"You think it's okay to sell the store, though? I mean, that's my grandparents' life. I don't want to let them down."

He wraps his arm around my back and pulls me into a side hug. "Evie, that was their life. They never expected it to be yours. They've always just wanted you to be happy. That's all. George would be so mad if he knew that you've been running the store even though it makes you unhappy."

"I was just thinking about him, actually," I confess.

Matt chuckles to himself. "Yeah, he was pretty amazing."

"That he was," I agree.

He pats my leg. "So, are you going to do it? Put the store up for sale. Start living your own dream?"

"Yeah." Hope lines my voice. "I am. Thank you, Matty. So much." I turn and wrap my arms around his back and hug him tight. "You're the best."

"Anytime, Evie. You know we're all here for you." He hugs me back.

Footsteps stop beside Matty and me in our embrace. "Ooh, it looks like I missed something good. What are you over here talking about?" Abby asks, her voice cheerful.

I release my hold on Matt. He pulls Abby down onto his lap and kisses her cheek.

"Matty helped me solve my midlife crisis." I grin toward my friends.

Abby throws her head back in laughter. "You are hardly midlife, babe. But I do want to know about this crisis. Do tell."

Hazel and a few of our other friends congregate around me, and I tell them the new plan. With each word, my chest feels lighter, and by the time I'm done talking, I feel more like myself than I have in a long time, and it feels great.

Chapter Three

Evie - 10 Years Old

The kitchen is sweltering as Sweetie fries up some potato slices on the stovetop. She's making one of my favorite meals—"Carrot" hot dogs, Brussels sprout, and fried potatoes. All of my friends love to tease me when I tell them that my favorite meal is hot dogs made of carrots, but I'm serious when I say they're delicious. Sweetie takes long, thick carrots and marinates them in some secret sauce for a couple of days and then cooks them up. Pops said they taste similar to real meat hot dogs, but I wouldn't know as I've never had that kind.

"Evie dear, can you please open a window? It's getting hot in here," my nana says.

"Sure." I open the back window that looks out to a parking lot behind our building. Across from the parking lot is an old church made with big stones. Pops said it is one of the very first buildings built in this town. I absolutely love it because it reminds me of an old castle. I used to put my Belle princess dress on and run around the church's perimeter, pretending I was fighting off the invaders of my kingdom. I won that game every time because there wasn't an evil knight I couldn't beat.

My grandparents tell me I can do anything, and I believe them.

I'm not sure what I want to be when I grow up, but whatever I do, I'm going to be fantastic at it. Unfortunately, there isn't a position for a butt-kicking princess in Cherry Blossom Grove, but something interesting is bound to come up. Whatever I decide to do, I'm never leaving my home. In a lot of the TV shows, I watch kids talking about growing up and moving away from home, but I never want to leave this town. I love it here. Most days, people come from all over just to see our town, so obviously, it's special.

The winters are busy with skiers who take advantage of the nearby ski slopes. Autumn brings people who want to see the vibrant colors of the changing leaves, and the cherries, of course, bring in the summer crowd. Early spring has the least number of visitors, but as soon as the cherry trees start blooming, the visitors start arriving.

I like the tourists. They're fun and usually so happy to be here. Plus, we own a candy shop, so it helps my family to have new people come through.

"When is Pops coming up?" I call from the window.

"Any minute. Can you set the table, please," Sweetie asks.

"Sure." I skip over to the china cabinet and pull out three plates. I've decided to fancy up the table for tonight's meal. Pops always said that every day is a reason for celebration. Sweetie made my favorite meal, and my two best friends are coming over tonight for a sleepover, so it's definitely a special day.

My grandparents got these dishes as their wedding present, and someday, when I get married, Sweetie will give them to me.

I set the table with the floral dishes and put out crystal wine glasses instead of our normal cups. Then I light the candles in the center of the table.

Sweetie comes into the dining room with the serving dishes. "Oh, so fancy. I love it, Evie. Can you go grab the condiments, please?"

I hurry to the kitchen and come back with the ketchup and mustard while Sweetie brings in the rest of the food. I pull a few cloth napkins out of the hutch and try to remember how to fold them into swans, but when I can't, I just roll them up and place them across the plates.

The kitchen door opens, and Pops comes in.

"Where are my girls?" he shouts as he shuts the door behind him. When he enters the dining room, he's carrying two bouquets of licorice sticks in his hands. One with a giant satin purple ribbon and a larger bouquet with a satin pink ribbon.

"Oh, my." Sweetie giggles. "What's the special occasion?"

He hands her the larger of the bouquets. "Every day is a special occasion, my beautiful wife." He leans in and kisses her.

"I was just thinking that!" I exclaim. "I even set the table like a holiday."

He turns to me and hands me the licorice sticks with the purple ribbon. "And that, Evie love, is why you and I are kindred spirits." He points at his temple with his forefinger, then presses it against my forehead. "We think alike." He shoots me a wink.

"Now before we see who gets the wishes, you need to think about what you're going to wish for," he tells us.

"If I get the wish stick, I'm wishing for a pony. Hazel just got a pony," I say.

Sweetie chuckles. "Well, Hazel also lives on a farm with lots of land."

"Pops says that if your wish is your deepest heart's desire, then it will come true," I remind her.

Pops looks at me. "That is true, but sometimes, what we think we want may not actually be what we want, so in that case, the wish wouldn't come true because it's not your true heart's desire." He nods toward the sticks of candy in my hand, asking if I'm ready.

"Yes!" I hold out my bouquet, and Pops stands across from me.

"Okay, pick."

I pull out a licorice stick, and it's a full-sized piece. *Darn.* Pops squints his eyes, studying the pieces of candy, and then he pulls out a long stick. I go again. *Long.* Pops goes. *Long.* I go. *Long.* Pops goes. *Long.* I go. *Short!*

"I got it," I yell, jumping up and down.

Sweetie claps, a wide smile on her face.

"All right, make your wish," Pops says.

I think about my pony wish, but I'm hesitant to make it. Do I really want a pony? Where would I keep it? In the parking lot? That wouldn't work. I guess I could ask Hazel's parents if my pony could live there, but how often would I be able to see it? And it's not really fair of me to make Hazel feed and water my pony every day. That's a lot of work. Plus, if I couldn't see my pony every day, I would miss it, and I'm sure it would miss me.

So, instead, I close my eyes and think, *I wish to have the most fun sleepover ever tonight.*

When I open my eyes, Pops asks, "Was it a good one?"

I nod.

He goes over to Sweetie and repeats the process. Sweetie pulled the short licorice stick on the second try. She closes her eyes and makes her wish. I'm dying to know what she wished for, but I don't ask. Wishes are always a secret.

When she's finished wishing, she gives Pops a kiss and thanks him for the bouquets.

"It smells delicious." Pops motions toward the table. "Let's eat."

We sit down to dinner, and Pops tells us about his

day down in the shop. I love listening to his stories. He always gets so excited and swings his hands around as he's talking. It makes me laugh.

After dinner, Pops says he has to take care of some things downstairs. Sweetie offers to do dishes even though it's my turn. "Can you just tidy up the bathroom before your friends get here?" she asks me.

"Sure," I say and hurry toward the bathroom. I hate washing the dishes. I'd rather do any chore instead of dishes, including cleaning a toilet.

After I finish cleaning the bathroom, I wash my hands and make my way out to the living room. The girls should be here any minute. Sweetie hands me a pile of movies. "Here. Take these down to your pops."

I look at the stack in my hand, and it's literally a pile of all of the movies I've been wanting to rent from the local movie store. "Are these for me?" I ask, shocked.

"Just take them downstairs. Your pops will show you what to do with them."

"Okay," I say slowly, confused.

I walk down the steps to the shop and gasp when I see the room. There are little multicolored lights strung around the room, the kind of lights on a Christmas tree. Pops has the floor in the front of the store covered in blankets. Three sleeping bags and pillows are laid on top of the blankets. The TV from our living room is set up with the VCR on a small table in front of the blankets.

Abby and Hazel stand next to Pops by the last row of candy.

"What do you think?" Pops asks, his arm extended toward the setup.

"I think this is incredible!" I giggle and run over to Pops, throwing my arms around him. "We can sleep down here?"

"Absolutely." He hugs me back.

I hug Abby and Hazel.

"This will be so much fun!" I say.

"Yeah, I brought games, too." Hazel holds up a couple of boxes.

"We are going to stay up all night playing games, watching movies, and talking about everything!" Abby shrieks, clapping her hands.

"You might need these," Sweetie says from behind me. I turn around, and she hands me some bowls.

"What are these for?" I ask.

"Movie snacks, of course." She grins.

"We can have whatever we want?" My gaze shoots toward my best friends, who are giggling by the table.

"Whatever you want. Just don't get sick. If your belly starts hurting, stop eating. Okay, girls?"

"Okay, Ms. Sweetie!" Abby and Hazel nod in agreement.

Sweetie motions toward the back counter by the cash register. "There is a pitcher of water over there and some cups if you get tired of drinking root beer."

"Okay!" I say.

"You girls are welcome to sleep down here, but you also can come upstairs anytime you want. If you get

scared in the middle of the night and want to sleep in
Evie's room, come on up," Sweetie reassures us.

I scoff. "We won't get scared."

"Well, if you do..." Sweetie leans in and gives me a
kiss on the forehead. "Love you."

"Love you, too, Evie." Pops kisses my head before
waving. "Have fun, girls!"

"Thank you!" we say in unison.

My grandparents walk upstairs.

"What should we watch first?" Abby asks.

"*The Lizzie McGuire Movie*, please! I've been
wanting to watch that forever," Hazel pleads.

"That works for me." I pull the tape out of the case
and push it into the VCR. "Go fill up your bowls!"

Abby and Hazel run around the shop, deciding what
candy to start with. I fill my bowl with chocolate-covered
raisins and gummy bears. They are my nana's two
favorite movie treats, so I feel like I should start with
them. It's tradition.

With our cups filled with root beer and our bowls
filled with candy, we set up the pillows so we can lean
against them. And with all the lights off, except the little
light strings, I start the movie.

We laugh, and gossip, and eat until our stomachs
ache.

It's the most fun sleepover, ever.

Chapter Four

Pumpkin purrs on Nana's lap beside me, and I love it. That cat won't give me the time of day, but he's always loved her. I'm glad for it.

"Evelyn dear, what are you looking at?" Nana asks me about the book in my lap. I know when she calls me Evelyn that she thinks I'm her daughter. Though I carry the same name as my mother, I've always been called Evie.

I scoot over next to my grandmother on the couch so she can see the book. "It's the scrapbook I made after the funeral for Pops."

I'm hesitant to show her because most days she doesn't remember losing him, and I don't want to cause her pain. Though I'm praying that she comes back to me today, if only for a moment. I need her.

I have an interested buyer meeting me down in the

shop in a little bit, and I could use some reassurance from her that I'm doing the right thing.

I gently urge Pumpkin off her lap, and he meows, annoyed. I set the book on her legs and wait as she looks at the pictures. I took so many photos on the day of his funeral. I captured the flowers, the setup, and the faces of those who came to celebrate my grandpa's life. Snapping the photos brought me solace on one of the hardest days of my life.

The book is on the depressing side, understandably, yet it also brings me a lot of comfort. Not to sound boastful, but the photos captured are quite stunning. So much beauty can be found in darkness, in the pain of life. Yes, losing my pops was a great loss. But the beautiful images from that day were also healing. The tears, the grief, and the sorrow can be felt radiating from the images. but they're not alone. They're accompanied by love, laughter, and gratitude for all the greatness that George Emberton brought to the world. My pops was loved deeply by so many. He lived every day of his life to the fullest, and it showed in the faces of those who came to say their goodbyes. Death is never easy, but knowing that the person was cherished by so many is a gift. Knowing he died happy and loved is a blessing that not everyone gets.

Nana runs her finger over the page of photos. I wait anxiously for her reaction. She sighs and turns the page. A small gasp comes from her lips when she sees the photos of the licorice bouquets. My pops used to surprise her with bouquets of red licorice sticks tied together with a ribbon. They had a game where they would take turns pulling pieces of licorice out of the bouquet, and the one who pulled the licorice stick with the shortened end would get to make a wish. Pops swore that licorice wishes were the strongest wishes out there. He said they were more powerful than wishing on a shooting star. Nana would always pull the shortened candy. Later when I came along, and I was gifted the red candy bouquets, I would pull the wish stick. Pops never got it, but that was by design.

Her frail, wrinkled hand reaches toward the photo and traces the edges. "Evie," she whispers.

"Sweetie?" My emotion lodged in my throat, I swallow.

She turns to me, her eyes filled with tears. "Evie?"

I wrap my arms around her and hug her to me. "You're here," I whisper against her favorite cream cardigan.

"I'm here, my girl." She rubs my back.

"I'm selling the shop, Sweetie. I'm sorry. I...there's just been so much to do...and I..." My words falter. I don't know how much time I have with her, and I need to tell her so much.

I sit back. Her lucid stare captures mine, and she takes my hands in her. "I am so proud of you, Evie."

"It's okay that I sell it?"

"Of course, my darling. It is not your burden to bear. That was your grandfather's and my happy place. It doesn't mean it's yours. You have to live your life for you."

My heart aches at her words and these stolen moments.

"Are you happy? Are you okay? Scared? Is there anything else I can do for you?" I ask her questions in rapid succession.

"I'm fine, dear. I'll be fine." She traces her thumb across my cheek and wipes an errant tear. "You look older. You're worrying too much."

"I don't want to let you down," I whisper.

She shakes her head. "You never could."

"I love you so much."

"I love you more."

We fall into another embrace. She pats my back as I tell her about the meeting coming up. "I guess this company specializes in buying small shops and boutiques in tourist towns and revamping the brand and marketing strategies to increase profits. Once I told my friends that I was thinking about selling, word got out. He was in town looking at Mrs. Miller's jewelry store, and he heard about us. It's happening quicker than I thought it would."

Her arms fall, and I sit back. She blinks a few times, and when she focuses again on my face, a stranger stares back.

"Sweetie?" I ask hesitantly.

"Evelyn dear, I'm feeling tired. I think I'm going to lie down." She pats my knee before standing.

My shoulders fall. "Okay, sounds good." I plaster on a tight smile and press my trembling lips together, willing to keep the tears at bay. I clear my throat and pull in a breath. "Actually, Christine is going to be here any minute. She'll be here if you need anything while I'm down at the shop."

"I don't need someone here. I have George," she answers and tosses the crocheted blanket that was across her lap onto the rocking chair.

"I know, but she likes hanging out here."

"Well, that's fine. All are welcome, of course," she says as she walks toward her bedroom.

White rag in hand, I shine the candy display again. The entire shop is pristine. Taking a step back, I admire my work.

"Looks pretty good," I say to Pumpkin, who rubs up against my feet.

I walk to the front of the store where our cherry table resides. It's the first thing that customers see when they walk in, a display with every cherry-flavored candy one could imagine, including my personal favorite, cherry-flavored chocolate. On both sides of the table are plastic rack cardholders with brochures for Abby's orchard, Hazel's vineyard, Matty's Mexican restaurant, and a handful of other tourist favorites. Everyone in town is so supportive of everyone else. It's a great community.

I pull out the Cherry Blossom Grove Orchard pamphlets and tap them against the table, ensuring they are all stacked together evenly before placing them back in the display.

The bell above the door sounds, and I turn to find a man, not much older than myself, walking in. He's tall, brunette, and quite handsome. Giving the fact that he's alone and wearing a suit, I know he's here for me.

"Hi. Welcome to Sweet as Pie." I grin.

He smiles wide. "Thank you. You must me Evie Emberton? I'm Hayes Watson. These are for you." He hands me a bouquet of multicolored lollipops.

"Suckers?" I say softly, taken aback.

"Yeah." Hayes shakes his head. "Is that weird?" He quirks up an eyebrow. "I'm sorry, I thought it would be fun, given you own a candy shop. I suppose I should've just gone status quo and brought flowers like a normal person." He chuckles to himself.

"No." I hold the bouquet against my chest. "I love them. It just made me think of my grandparents, the original owners of this place. My pops used to always bring my nana bouquets of candy, licorice mainly."

"Licorice?" His full lips tilt up into a grin. "That's a new one."

"Yeah, well, my pops was one of kind. Anyway, I think the gesture is sweet. Thank you." I nod toward the candy in my grasp.

"I didn't want to come empty-handed. It's already awkward walking into these meetings where we discuss my company buying your business. I do this a lot, and I know these businesses are the people's life work. I appreciate the gravity of a business owner in the position of selling something they created. I know it's not easy to sell, and as much as I'm probably seen as the bad guy, I want you to know it's not my intention to be."

"Thank you. I appreciate that. And you're right. It's not easy. My grandparents moved from a bigger city in Southern Michigan to start this shop sixty years ago because they fell in love with this town. I've been here my whole life. In fact, we live right above here." I point up toward our apartment. "It breaks my heart to sell, but I know it's the right thing to do."

"Well, I'd love to hear a little bit about the place from your perspective. Can we start with the name? Where did Sweet as Pie come from? According to my research, you don't sell pies. Correct?"

"That's correct." I chuckle. "That was also my pops. He called my nana Sweetie because from the moment he met her, she was sweet as pie. Also, I think he did it to be funny. He used to love when tourists came in looking for a cherry pie and left with pounds of candy instead."

"That's kind of a brilliant business move," Hayes says with a grin.

"He was smart. I think one has to have some solid business skills to be able to make a good living selling processed sugar." I chuckle.

"Well, as I mentioned on the phone, our company is housed in New York. And even there, your little town

here is very well-known as a must-see small-town desti-
nation. You all have managed to create something really
special here. Besides the obvious draw of the cherries or
orchards, Sweet as Pie is a tourist favorite. I heard you
have the best root beer floats in the world?" He puckers
his lips and raises a brow, causing me to laugh.

"I don't know about the world, but they are pretty
amazing." I lead him toward the back of the store.
"Come on. I'll make one for you."

"So candy and root beer floats? Anything else?
Other ice creams?" he asks as he follows me.

"No, Pops always said that less is more and to make
what you do the best. Truthfully, I think he originally
started selling root beer floats because a family friend
needed help. My friend Elijah's family runs a dairy farm
on the other side of town. Years ago, their business was
really struggling, so Pops went to them with the idea to
use their ice cream. They make the ice cream that we
use in the floats. It's amazing. So creamy and rich. It's
unlike any vanilla ice cream that you'd find in a store.
We also use root beer from a Michigan vendor." I scoop
some ice cream into the glass and fill it with the fizzy
brown soda. "The final touch is a few drops of pure
quality vanilla." I squeeze the dropper of vanilla into
Hayes's glass. "My grandfather always called it the
secret ingredient, but then always added it at the end
right in front of the customer, so it's not real secret." I
chuckle and hand Hayes the dessert.

He uses the long-handled spoon and takes a bite.

"That's really good." He nods before taking a sip of the root beer from the straw.

"Right? It's delicious. The funny thing is, I'm not even a huge fan of root beer by itself but mixed with the ice cream and vanilla, it's amazing. One of my favorite things."

"I'm impressed. I never thought I would go somewhere just for a root beer float, but I'd travel a good distance for another one of these," he says.

"Thanks. You can finish that while I show you around." I point toward the glass in his hand.

"Sounds good."

I walk Hayes around the shop and point out the different candies that we have and the way we package them. Almost everything we do now was done from the beginning. A part of the charm of the place is that it still feels like a candy shop from sixty years ago. The adventure is in the simplicity of everything from the concept to the packaging. Life nowadays is complicated and busy. People come here to escape from the hustle and bustle of everyday life. It's incredible what a plain white bag of treats handpicked from our glass display cases can do to lift one's spirits. No one leaves Sweet as Pie without a smile on their face.

As I explain our shop's concept and philosophy in detail to Hayes, I feel my grandfather's presence. He told me the same things when I was growing up. He was so proud of this place, and rightfully so. It really is a little piece of heaven on earth.

Chapter Five

Hazel wraps the curling iron around my red hair and holds it before releasing it. The long locks fall in ringlets.

"Your hair is so easy to work with. I love it curled," she says.

I texted Hazel earlier to tell her about my business dinner tonight with Hayes Watson, and she insisted on coming to help me get ready. She loves hair, makeup, and fashion. We always tease her that she should be living somewhere glamorous out in California. She'd fit right in out in LA. She's movie-star gorgeous with her long, shiny ebony hair and her sky-blue eyes. Her beauty is striking, and she's always dressed to perfection. Even when she's working, she could be in a photoshoot for the vineyard.

My signature style is much different. My clothes are simplistic, and my hair is usually up in a ponytail tied with a ribbon bow. Nana always tied ribbons in my hair and it kind of stuck. Plus, I always felt the ribbon was charming and fit in with the feel of the shop.

"Just a little," I tell her as she pulls out her makeup bag.

"I know." Her voice is reassuring. "Just a little mascara and blush to emphasize your perfect features."

"I want to look like myself," I say.

"You will. Yourself but a little better." She grins.

"Hazel," I groan.

"I'm kidding. You're always perfect. But seriously...a tad of mascara will make your gorgeous greens pop." She swipes my eyelashes with the mascara wand. "So, tell me more about this date."

"It's not a date," I correct her. "It's a business dinner."

"Yeah, okay." She laughs.

"What?" My voice rises an octave in question.

"So, he's hot as you not so subtly mentioned. He's about our age. He's sweet, charming, and funny. He asked you out and based on the black dress you're wearing, I'd say you want to impress. So, it's a date."

"I'm wearing this dress because it's professional," I argue.

"And sexy."

"No, professional."

"Whatever you say, girl. I'm just saying you should have fun. You deserve it." Hazel teases my locks with her fingers, breaking up the spiraled curls into waves.

"Listen. Yes, he's cute," I admit. "And all of the other things you said. But he's here to make the offer on the shop, then he's headed back to New York. There's no point in making this more than it is. I want to look good tonight so he takes me seriously and offers us a good price. That's all. Pretending this is anything else is silly."

"Fine," Hazel relents. "It's just fun pretending. I can't even remember the last time you went on a date."

"Gosh, I know. Was it with Elijah senior year?" I rack my brain and I can't come up with another date I've gone on since graduating high school seven years ago.

"No! Your last date was not senior prom with Eli?" Hazel shrieks.

I pinch my face into a grimace. "I think it was. How can that be?"

Hazel presses her forearm to her forehead in dramatic fashion. "I can't believe this."

"I know. What is wrong with me?" I ask in all seriousness.

She shakes her head and continues fussing with my hair. "Well, you've had a lot going on with your grandpa's death, Sweetie's health, and running the shop by yourself."

"Yeah but still..." I sigh.

"I know," Hazel agrees. "Listen, the first thing we're doing after you sell the shop is get you a date. So, you're going to show up tonight as sexy, I mean professional, as can be and get a great offer, sell the shop, and start your new life."

"Sounds like a plan."

"Where are you taking him anyway?" Hazel wonders.

"Amigos."

"Evie," Hazel chastises. "Amigos? You're going to close the sale at a Mexican restaurant? Why not Clara's? It's quiet, classy, and is better suited for a professional meeting."

"I know, but I wanted to support Matty's parents," I tell her.

"You're too loyal for your own good." She blows out a breath and steps back. "Well, you're absolute perfection. My work here is done."

"Thanks."

"Go get him."

* * *

The patio outside Amigos is scattered with pink flower petals. The trees lining the courtyard threw a party and dropped their confetti, leaving bright green leaves in their wake, a sign that summer has officially come to Northern Michigan. Despite the winters being a little longer and harsher than I'd like, Michigan is a beautiful place to live. Every season brings its own magic.

"Evie," a husky timbre greets me.

"Hayes, hello."

He's changed out of his gray suit from earlier and into a black one. His pastel pink button-up shirt makes me smile. He radiates confidence and fun at the same time. I take a moment to really look at him in the daylight. Day-old scruff covers his chiseled jaw, and it somehow makes his bright brown eyes pop even more. He's styled his short brown hair to perfection without looking wet or hardened by product. He smiles wide as he takes me in, and I can't help but blush. He's so dapper —he'd be perfect for the cover of GQ magazine.

I know this dinner is purely business, and after he signs the paperwork, he's going to leave town, but I can't help the butterflies that dance in my belly. This meeting is the closest thing I've had to a date in years and it's invigorating.

"You look beautiful," he tells me.

"Thanks. You, too." I shake my head. "I mean, nice. You look nice."

He chuckles. "Thanks. Shall we?" He motions toward the restaurant.

"Yes." I smile and lead the way.

After we're seated, he looks around at the colorful décor of the restaurant. "This looks fun. I have to say I was a little surprised that you picked this place."

"Why's that?"

"Usually, when people find out my company is covering the bill for dinner, they choose the most expen-sive place in town. Looking online today at the different restaurants, I figured you'd pick Clara's." He opens his menu.

"Yeah, well Mexican food is my favorite, and this

place has the most delicious authentic Mexican food around. Plus, one of my best friend's parents owns this place, so I like to give them business when I can." I nod toward the menu. "I swear, it's all amazing. You can't go wrong with any of it."

A basket of tortilla chips and a carafe of salsa with two small bowls are set on the table between Hayes and me.

"Welcome to Amigos," Matty's cheerful voice greets us.

"Hey! I was just talking about you," I say. "Hayes, this is my friend Matteo Fernandez. His parents own the restaurant." I look up to address Matt. "Matty, this is Hayes Watson. His company is looking into purchasing the shop."

Matt extends his hand toward Hayes. "Matt. Nice to meet you."

Hayes shakes his hand. "Pleasure to meet you, Matt."

"I didn't know you were working today," I say.

"Yeah, Florence called in, so I came in to help out. Plus, I figured I'd better help while I can. Things over at Abby's place are about to get crazy."

I speak to Hayes. "Matty works at the cherry orchard, and it's basically a madhouse for two months straight during cherry season."

"Oh, I guess it would be," Hayes remarks.

"What can I get you to drink?" Matt asks.

"I'll just take a water, please," I say.

"Just a water?" Hayes raises an eyebrow. "You can order anything you'd like." He looks toward the bar. "I bet they have great margaritas."

"Yeah, they do." I press my lips into a smile. "Fine. I'll take a margarita as well, please."

"I'll have the same," Hayes says.

"Sounds good." Matt nods before leaving us to put in the drink order.

"You really surprise me, Evie," Hayes says.

"Why do you say that?"

"I don't know. I guess I'm just used to working with people who take advantage of others. You're so giving and kind." He squints his eyes as he takes me in.

"That's not rare, though. At least not here. We all look out for one another."

"Maybe." He shrugs. "It's definitely rare from my experience." He scans the menu. "How are the fajitas?"

"Incredible." I grin.

"I figured you'd say that." He smirks.

Matt drops off our drinks and takes our orders.

"So let's get the business talk out of the way, shall we?" Hayes suggests.

"Sure," I say as my heart beats rapidly within my chest.

"My company is interested in buying it." He slides a paper across the table with a figure, and my chest swells because it's more than I had hoped for. "But we want to go into this sale a little differently than others."

I take a sip of the margarita. "Okay," I say hesitantly,

my gaze dropping to the large number typed out on the paper before I look back up at Hayes.

"You see, a candy shop is somewhat of a risky investment. I've gone over your paperwork and business tax returns and I have to say that Sweet as Pie has done really well. Compared to stores similar to yours, you've surpassed them all with incredible profits. But I don't think that's simply a result of your product. There's so much more that goes into it. I'd like to stay and work with you for the next month so I can see how your business is run, how you work with customers and vendors, how you advertise...all of it. You and your grandparents have created this enchanted little place, and I want to learn how you do it so that we can duplicate it once we take over."

"Um, sure. That seems reasonable. That's probably common practice. I mean, you'd want to know that it will still be a profitable business once you take over, and I can understand that. Will you be the one staying to run it?" I ask.

"No. I will work with you over the next month to watch and learn, and then I'll create a training program by which we'll train our future employees. And actually, we've never done this. Sales are usually closed pretty quickly. I've never stayed back like this before, but I really do think there is something special about your shop. I believe it is a good investment and want to ensure my bosses that it will be profitable going forward."

"Okay, sounds good," I say with a grin.

"Great." He raises his margarita. "Cheers to a successful collaboration."

I tap my margarita glass with his. "Cheers."

Hayes Watson is going to work side by side with me for the next month. That thought both terrifies and exhilarates me. Suddenly, the stress of work doesn't seem that heavy.

Chapter Six

"I have a Q, U, I, and Z," I say as I place my tiles down on the Scrabble board between Nana and me. "That's twenty-two points plus the triple word score, making it sixty-six." I jot down the score on a pad of paper at my side.

"Hmm. That's a good one," Nana says, tapping her pointer finger against her lips as she looks at her tiles.

Nana, Pops, and I have played Scrabble ever since I could spell. It's always been one of our favorite games. Nana can no longer do or remember many things, but Scrabble isn't one of them, so I play it with her often.

"Well, it's not the best, but I'm going to use that Z and make zeal." She places the E, A, and L tiles down. "That's fifteen with the double letter on the L," she says. "Too bad we can't use that triple word tile twice."

I write down Nana's score. "I know. Remember how

Pops would change the rules every time? He was such a cheat." I chuckle.

She smiles and draws three new tiles from the bag. "That he was. Where is your father?" She looks around the room with worry etched on her face.

"He's out running errands," I say quickly. "Getting supplies."

Nana nods and releases a breath, once again content.

Several knocks sound from the entry door before Hazel and Abby walk in.

"Hey, ladies!" Hazel greets us. "Hi, Ms. Sweetie." She places a hand on Nana's shoulder.

Nana taps Hazel's hand. "Hello, dear."

"Ooh, Scrabble. Who's winning?" Abby asks.

"It's really close," I say. "I just got an awesome score, so I'm up by twenty, but I have a feeling Sweetie is coming back."

"Oh, you know I am." Nana grins.

"So, are we going to discuss the hottie down in the store all by himself?" Abby quirks her eyebrow.

"Who's in the store?" Nana asks.

"I hired someone to help out for a while," I reassure her. "I don't have the best letters. Let's do HIM for eight points." I place down the tiles. "I'm going to go feed Pumpkin. You have time to come up with an awesome high-point word while I'm gone."

Hazel and Abby follow me into the kitchen. The second I enter the kitchen, Pumpkin is at my feet meowing. I start opening his can of food.

"Wasn't the deal that Hayes works beside you for a month? It's the second day. Why is he down there without you?" Hazel asks.

I place the dish of cat food on the ground.

"He's doing inventory. I showed him how to do it. It's not really a two-person job." I shrug.

"Evie," Abby draws out my name in judgment.

"What?" I laugh. "It's not. Anyone can do inventory. Plus, the whole point of selling the shop is to spend more time with Sweetie and lighten my load a little. So I showed him how to do it, and I came up here."

"And that's the only reason?" Hazel puckers her lips.

I bite the inside of my cheek. "Well..."

"I knew it!" Abby laughs.

"What?" I feign confusion.

"You like him!" Abby says.

"Totally," Hazel chimes in.

"No." I shake my head. "I hardly know him. It's seriously been two days. It's not like that. It's just awkward having a shadow in the shop all day, and it's exhausting. If there's not a customer, I feel like I should be talking or showing him something. Coming up with things to talk about all of the time is tiring. You know? My brain needed a break." I rub my temples for effect. "And seriously, you two are ridiculous. There's no point in thinking about him in any way but professionally. He's here for work, and then he's leaving. A crush isn't going to change anything, so having one would be pointless."

"But...?" Abby urges, a mischievous smile on her face.

I sigh and press my lips together.

"But he does smell really good. It's kind of intoxicating," I admit.

"And?" Hazel urges, leaning in toward me.

I roll my eyes. "And he's exceptionally gorgeous... and nice, and funny, and...ugh!" I cover my face with the palms of my hand.

Hazel and Abby burst out in giggles.

"I knew it!" Abby cheers.

They exchange knowing looks, and their laughter subsides.

"You guys. It seriously doesn't matter what I think of him. He's leaving. And it's nothing. Really. We all know he's cute. There's no shame in admitting it." I shrug.

"There's definitely not," Hazels says. "And a month is a long time. You can have a lot of fun in a month. I mean, why not?"

I squint my eyes. "No. Absolutely not. Like I said, it's not like that. I just find him attractive. Gosh, have you two always been such gossips?" I chuckle.

"Well, when your friend's last crush was senior year of high school... gossiping is a must. Come on. We never get to tease you like this," Abby states, clapping her hands together.

"Yes. We need this," Hazel agrees.

"You two are crazy." I grin. "Anyway, was there

another reason you came over? Or did you legitimately come over to spy on Hayes?"

"Mainly to spy," Abby says. "Matty said that all of the female servers wouldn't stop ogling over him at the restaurant the other night, so I had to check him out for myself."

"And?" I ask.

"I think you're going to have an interesting month on your hands," Abby says.

"That's for sure," Hazel agrees.

"I'll be just fine," I say.

Abby raises an eyebrow. "We'll see. You've never been one for temptation."

I let out a laugh. "Seriously. What does that even mean? Now, you're just saying random things."

Hazel points a finger in my direction and nods. "No, she's right. You've never been able to turn down a hot fudge sundae when we go to Twisters even when you say you're not getting one."

"So! That's a dessert, not a person." I laugh.

Abby quirks an eyebrow. "I'd say it's the same concept."

The TV blares from the living room, and I poke my head in to see what Nana's up to. She's holding the remote control in her hand and must be pressing the volume button because the sound continues to get louder.

Jogging into the room, I take the remote from her

and turn down the TV. "Can I help you find a show, Sweetie?"

"Yes, dear. I'd like to watch the *Golden Girls*. Where is your father? You know he loves that show. That Rose is so funny." She grins.

I turn on the Blu-ray player and start the *Golden Girls* disc that I have ready at all times. This show is comforting to Nana. It turns out purchasing the series boxset has been a blessing and money well spent.

"I'm setting it up now. Do you want to finish the game?" I ask her.

"What game, dear?"

"Scrabble."

"You want to play Scrabble? I'm not sure I'm up to a game right now. Can we wait for your father to get back? Where is he?" She pets Pumpkin, and he crawls up onto her lap.

"He's running errands. He'll be back," I reassure her.

Bending down, I fold the Scrabble board and slide the tiles into the letter pouch, and put the rest of the pieces into the box. I feel guilty for leaving the game to go talk to my friends in the kitchen. It's the furthest Nana and I have gotten into the game in a long time. I was just afraid that my conversation with the girls would be startling to her. She wouldn't have understood it, and it could have set her off. But I was gone for too long, and she forgot. It's a shame to put away the board when we were so close to finishing, but I don't want Sweetie to look down at it and become upset because she doesn't remember playing in the first place. Life with my nana is like trying to balance a teeter-totter by myself. I'm standing in the middle, struggling to make sure that my weight is evenly distributed on both sides because if either side were to become too heavy, it would crash to the ground. And the falls are the worst.

I close the top of the game box and slide it onto the bottom shelf of the coffee table.

"Oh, this is a great episode," Abby states from beside me as she looks at the TV.

Nana turns her head toward Abby, a look of confusion in her eyes. "I'm sorry. We haven't met. I'm Edith Emberton, but you can call me Ms. Sweetie." She extends a hand out toward Abby.

Abby doesn't miss a beat. She leans down and shakes Nana's hand. "Hi, Ms. Sweetie. I'm a friend of Evie's."

"You must be new to town?" Nana says.

"You guessed it." Abby grins.

"Well, welcome! This is a wonderful place to live. You're going to love it here," she says before turning her attention toward the show.

We turn to head back toward the kitchen, and Nana calls after me. "Evelyn. Where's your father? He loves this show. He'd hate to miss it."

I look back and give my grandmother a smile. "He'll be back soon. Don't worry."

Chapter Seven

The bell chimes above the shop door, and one of my favorite people walks in—the Amazon delivery person, Tucker.

"Tucker, my favorite guy!" I exclaim and raise my hands in the air in a mock cheer, causing him to laugh.

"Oh, Evie. I bet you say that to all of the delivery people." He holds a blue and white padded envelope in his grasp.

I hold my head high. "Nope, only you."

"Unless FedEx or UPS come bearing gifts," he retorts.

"Still only you."

He sets the padded envelope down on the counter. "I don't believe you."

"Well, considering Emily is my normal FedEx girl, and Margot is my regular UPS lady, I wouldn't call them my favorite guy. Would I?" I pout out my lips.

"Fine." Tucker chuckles. "You get off on a technicality." He looks around. "Now, where's my favorite demon cat?"

"He's on the ground under the table over by the root beer cooler. He's mad at me for some reason." I nod toward the table.

"Are you depriving him of his wet food?"

I scoff. "Look at him. Does he look remotely deprived?"

"Just checking. You know I have to look out for my favorite cat." He reaches into his shirt pocket and pulls out a baggy of cat treats. Bending at the knee, he drops a couple of treats in front of Pumpkin. Then he pets Pumpkin's head, causing the orange fluff ball to whine in protest. "See, he loves me."

"That he does." I giggle.

I don't have the heart to tell Tucker that Pumpkin never eats the treats. They are basically pieces of dry cat food in the shape of fish. Pumpkin hates dry cat food. As soon as Tucker leaves, I'll end up throwing the pieces away.

"How's Karen?" I ask about his daughter. She's a little younger than me and living with Tucker and his wife. She's eight months pregnant and is going to raise the baby as a single mom. Her boyfriend left her when he found out she was expecting.

"Good. Getting bigger every day. The baby's doing great. I told you it was a boy, right?" He grins proudly.

"You did. That's so exciting." I step over to one of the

display cases and start to fill a white paper bag. "Here." I hand the bag to Tucker. "I packed some chocolate-covered pretzels in there for Karen. I know they are her favorite."

"You're too sweet," Tucker says. "I just hope they'll last the day." He shoots me a guilty look.

"Well, I also put a large scoop of chocolate-covered raisins in there for my favorite delivery guy to snack on today. I know they're your favorite." I wink.

"Thank you, Evie. You're the best." He peeks inside the bag and smiles. "Well, I better get going. Until next time." He waves.

I wave back. "Bye. Drive safe."

After Tucker leaves, I walk over to Pumpkin and pick up the treats. "You know, it wouldn't kill you to eat them at least once. You're so spoiled." I rub the soft fur under his chin, and he leans into my hand.

Standing, I toss the treats into the trash.

Hayes stares at me, his arms crossed over his chest as he leans against the storage room doorframe. An expression I can't place rests on his face.

"What?" I ask.

He shrugs and pushes off the wall. "You."

"Me? What about me?"

He steps toward the front counter. "You're just full of surprises. You know your delivery people's names?"

"Yeah, of course. Don't you?"

He lets out a chuckle. "I can honestly say that I've never known a delivery person's name."

"Well, it's different for you. You're from a big city. I'm sure you have lots of different people coming in and out. I have the same three. I would be pretty horrible if I didn't learn their names. Right?"

He shrugs. "Maybe. And how do you expect to make money by giving away all of your goods?"

"It's called customer service," I tease. "Well, that and being a good human."

"I agree, it's very nice and all, but how are you supposed to make money by doing that?" he questions.

"Look, I gave him a little bag of chocolate. Not a big deal. He's been my delivery man for years. He's a friend. Plus, whenever he needs something sweet, he orders from me. He gives his family little treat-filled goodie bags from my shop every Christmas. He ordered favor bags for his daughter's baby shower from me. He's a regular customer. The thing about small-town businesses is that it's not always about the bottom line every second of the day. It's about the people. I've invested in him and his family, and he's invested in mine. I show him I care, which I do. And in return, he uses me as his sugar dealer whenever the need arises. In small towns, we build connections and support each other. It all works out."

"Yeah, that makes sense. I just don't know how I'm going to incorporate that sentiment into the training plan." He waves his hand in front of him and starts speaking in a funny radio show announcer's voice, "All right, trainees. Here's the deal. Sometimes you give stuff away for free. Sometimes the customers pay. It all works out. Don't worry about it."

I laugh. "It's not really something you teach. It's a small-town way of life."

"So what you're saying is once you sign this place over to my firm, we're doomed?" he teases.

"Well, chances are the people you have working here will be local, so they'll get it on their own."

"Yeah, you see, Evie. It doesn't really work like that. You're the owner, so you're invested in customer service. When it comes to employees, though, there have to be company rules. It's not a good idea to just leave things up to employee discretion."

"I'm not sure what to tell you, Hayes," I say.

I understand what he's talking about, and I agree. Some things can't be taught, or perhaps the correct way to say it is they can't be taught in a two-hour new customer training program. Everything I learned about running this place came from my grandparents. I watched them for years growing up. I watched my pops put people first and foster a place that people come for a little slice of happiness. When customers enter our shop, they know they'll have a friendly face to talk to.

Hayes nods toward the package. "What'd you order?"

"Oh." I rip the top of the mailer off and pull out the package inside. "It's a new camera battery. The one I have now only holds a charge for like an hour." Reaching under the counter, I pull out my camera bag and open it. I place the new battery in the side pocket.

"What do you have here?" Hayes asks, pulling my camera from the bag. "A Canon Rebel?"

"It was a graduation present from my grandparents. I know it's not the best camera out there, but it really does take great photos."

"No, it's great. I have one of these, too. You like taking pictures?"

"Yeah, actually, once I sell the store, I want to make a business out of it. I used to take pictures all of the time. From freshman year in high school on, I'd always had a camera nearby. I love capturing emotions and the beauty of everyday life. I think I could do really well with weddings and family photo shoots."

Hayes nods. "Oh, definitely. If you get your name out there, you can make good money. This area seems ideal for those types of photos. You certainly have the scenery."

"Yeah, that's what I was thinking."

"Do you have a website, business cards, and a portfolio ready?"

I shake my head. "No, not yet. Gary is the local guy who helps me with the shop's website. He's on a month-long cruise right now, so I have to wait until he gets back."

"I can help you build a website for your photography business," Hayes offers.

"Really?"

"Of course. It'd be my pleasure. You should really be getting that stuff up and running now, maybe even get a few photoshoots in that you can use for your online portfolio." He turns the camera on and looks into the viewfinder, and turns the lens to focus.

"I know. I should. I've just been so busy."

"Well, I'd love to help you," he says again.

"You don't have to. I'm sure I can figure it out."

"Don't be silly. I'd love to. It'd be a great distraction from my boring hotel life after I leave here."

"What do you do when you leave here?"

He lowers the camera from his face. "Well, let's see. I go back to my hotel room. I usually pick up food on the way there. I eat, correspond with the main office, and research other possible businesses that we might acquire on my laptop. If I'm lucky, I fit in an episode of *Jeopardy*." He grins. "Not too exciting."

"I'm sorry," I say.

"For?" He narrows his eyes.

"I didn't even think about the fact that you go to the hotel and eat alone. I should have invited you up to eat with Sweetie and me."

"It's fine, Evie. Our arrangement doesn't include you feeding me." He chuckles.

"I know, but I feel horrible. I mean, I knew you were going back to the hotel after work, but I guess I've been so caught up in my own life that I didn't stop to think what that would entail. You don't know anyone in town, and you've been spending your evenings alone. I'm so sorry, Hayes."

"I'm good. Really. You seriously have nothing to feel guilty over. Truthfully, that's my life. I travel to new towns, scope out potential businesses, and spend my evenings in a hotel room working. That's just how it is. It's cool." He shrugs.

"Well, it's not good enough for me." I shake my head, dropping my gaze. "It's out of character for me. I should've invited you up the first day. Please just know that you are always welcome to eat and hang out with us every evening that you want. Full disclosure, we watch a lot of *Golden Girls,* so if that's an issue, you might not want to, but the invitation is always there."

"Thank you, Evie. And, please don't feel bad. I've only been here four days, definitely not long enough to question your small-town hospitality or lack thereof." He smirks, his big browns capture my greens, and I can't look away.

"Well..." I clear my throat. "You're coming over tonight. I'm making tacos."

"Sounds good."

He lifts my camera up to his face and snaps a picture of me.

"What are you doing?" I ask.

"Just checking your camera and making sure it works. Stay still." He zooms in and takes another picture.

"It works just fine," I grumble.

"I'll be the judge of that." He continues to take pictures of me from different angles.

After a minute, he stops and looks down at the camera. Pressing the back arrow, he looks through the pictures he's just taken.

He nods as his eyes squint in concentration. "Yeah," he says slowly.

"What?"

"You're right. The camera works great. The pictures are..." He pauses and stares into my eyes. "Beautiful." Extending his arm, he hands me the camera. "What time is dinner?"

"What?" I swallow the lump in my throat.

"Tacos?" He quirks an eyebrow. "What time?"

"Oh." I blink a couple of times, clearing my head. "Ummm... seven o'clock."

He grabs his laptop bag from the counter. "Okay, sounds good. I have a video conference call in a bit, so I have to head out a little early. But I'll see you then?"

"Okay," I answer softly.

He gifts me a small smile, and then he's gone, leaving me to wonder what just happened and why I'm suddenly feeling unsettled.

Several seconds after the shop door closes behind him, I peer down toward the camera in my grasp. My face is on the display screen. I wear a small smile and a curious expression in the candid photo. The lighting and angle of the shot are perfect. It's a good picture of me, I'll give him that.

Chapter Eight

I pull the roasted vegetables out of the oven, and they smell delicious. I toss a spicy cauliflower piece into my mouth and immediately regret it as the scorching hot vegetable burns the top of my mouth.

"Ouch," I moan before taking a long chug of water.

Have I not learned anything in my twenty-five years? *Patience.* I've never been able to wait to taste test delicious food. It's a character flaw that I inherited from my pops. Nana used to call us silly fools because we insisted on taste testing all the baked goodies right out of the oven. In our defense, Sweetie was the best cook in the entire world.

Seriously—in the entire world.

She loses pieces of herself every day, and I miss them all. Her culinary skills are no exception. She no longer cooks or bakes, and I miss it. She taught me well over the years, and the meals I prepare are decent, but I don't think I'll ever be as good as she was.

A light knock sounds on the door. I toss the oven mitt onto the counter and step toward the door. It's just tacos, I remind myself. Not a big deal.

Turning the knob, I open the door to find Hayes standing there with his arms full of beverages. "Hi." I chuckle as I look at the items in his grasp. "What is all of that?" I question and stand to the side to allow him in.

He enters and unloads the bottles onto the counter. "I know." He shakes his head with a laugh. "Well, I knew you were making tacos, so I thought maybe tequila?" He hands me a bottle of Patrón and a plastic jug of margarita mix. "Then I thought that might be weird, given that it's just a normal Wednesday night dinner with your nana, and maybe you two aren't liquor drinkers. So then I thought about wine." He hands me a glass bottle of sangria. "Then I wondered what if you and your nana aren't drinkers at all, so I also brought pop, both caffeinated"—he holds out a two-liter of Coke —"and non." He shows me the two-liter of Sprite.

"You're ridiculous." I grin. "You didn't have to bring anything."

"It's polite to bring something when someone invites you to dinner, and since you literally live atop a giant room of sweets, I didn't think dessert was ideal, so I went with drinks."

"That you did." I shake my head. "Well, thank you, and actually, my nana loves Coca-Cola. It was one of my grandpa's favorite drinks. I don't ever buy it, so she'll be thrilled."

I grab three tall glasses from the cupboard and fill them with ice. I pour Coke into the first two. "Do you want pop or maybe a tall glass of the tequila?" I quirk up a brow.

"Coke is fine." Hayes grins.

"So, I told you that I'm selling the shop to spend more time with my nana and to focus on photography, but I should tell you she has Alzheimer's, so some of the things she says may not make sense. First, she thinks I'm my mother, Evelyn, and she thinks my pops is still alive."

"I'm so sorry, Evie. That must be so hard." Hayes grabs my hand.

I look down at where our hands meet, and he lets go. "It is," I say. "But it's okay too because at least she isn't afraid. In the beginning, I would remind her who I am and go over the fact that both her daughter and husband are gone, but it was horrible watching her relive that grief every day. It was truly heartbreaking. At least right now, she's happy and still remembers something from her life. I know soon that will be gone too."

Hayes stares down at me, his eyes assessing. There's a thought on the tip of his tongue, I can feel it. I decide that this casual dinner has already taken a turn toward depressing, so I speak before he can.

"Anyway..." I wave my hand through the air. "Can you help me carry some of this out to the table?" I motion toward the plated components of the meal.

"Sure." Hayes picks up the tortilla warmer. "Everything smells amazing. What kind of tacos did you make?" He grabs the bowl of seasoned beans.

"Veggie tacos. Nana and I are vegetarians. I promise you're going to love them. You won't even miss the meat." I take hold of two serving dishes and lead the way into the dining room.

"When we ate at Amigos, you said that everything on the menu was delicious. You haven't even eaten most of the food there, have you?" he questions with a smirk.

"No, but I know it's all amazing. Your meal was incredible, right?"

"Well, yeah." He follows me into the dining room.

"There you go," I say in response.

"Sweetie, dinner is ready. It's taco night," I call into the living room as I set the dishes in my hand down on the table. "Can you grab the glasses of Coke from the kitchen, please?" I ask Hayes.

I find my grandmother sleeping in her recliner in front of the TV, which is playing an infomercial about a vacuum with a thousand different functions. Nana and I watched the same show about the vacuum the other night, and it took everything I had not to call in with my credit card number and pay the one hundred and ninety-nine dollar payment every month for six months.

I'm hesitant to wake her, but she takes a few of her medications before bed, and she can't take them on an empty stomach. Plus, taco night is her favorite.

"Sweetie." I bend down and tap her arm. "Wake up. It's time to eat." She starts to stir, and I stand.

She opens her eyes and blinks several times before looking up at me.

"Time to eat," I say again.

Her eyes go wide, and she stares at me. I extend my hand to help her up. "We have a guest, and he brought you something special."

She turns her head from side to side, taking in her surroundings. "Who are you? Where am I?" she finally asks.

"You are Edith Emberton, but everyone calls you Ms. Sweetie. You are home and safe. Come eat something. You'll feel better," I reassure her.

"Get away from me," she warns me.

"Sweetie. It's me. You're home. It's okay."

She picks up a porcelain duck that sits on the end table beside her and throws it. It smashes against the window, cracking the glass. I step back with a gasp, covering my mouth with my hands. Tears fill my eyes. I've been warned she might become violent as she forgets, but this is the first time. My heart hammers in my chest as I try to figure out what I should do.

"I said leave me alone!" she yells. "I don't know you. You're not taking me anywhere!"

My lip trembles as tears flow down my cheeks. My heart is breaking.

I startle when Hayes steps to my side. I had momentarily forgotten he was here. "I don't know what to do," I tell him. "I don't know," I repeat, swiping the back of my hand across my cheek to wipe the tears. "I'm going to call her nurse," I say before handing him the Blu-ray remote. "Here. Play the disc. Maybe the familiarity of it will calm her."

The nurse picks up, and I explain what's going on. She tells me which medications to give Sweetie to calm her down. I thank her and grab the pills and the glass of Coke. I find Nana quietly watching the *Golden Girls* in the living room. Hayes sits on the sofa and watches along.

"Sweetie?" I question, my voice hesitant. She looks at me but doesn't say anything. "It's time to take your medicine, and Hayes brought some Cola-Cola." I hold up the glass to show her.

"That's my husband's favorite," she says.

"Yes, it is." I smile and hand her the pills and glass of soda.

I let out a sigh when she takes the medicine without a fight. I sit down beside Hayes and watch my grandmother as she smiles at her show and sips her cola. Despite the awkwardness of the past few minutes, I'm thankful Hayes is here. His presence is forcing me to hold it together. Inside, my soul weeps. I'm terrified if I let the sadness out, I'd never stop crying.

After a few moments, Sweetie looks at me. "Evelyn dear, I'm tired."

"Okay." Relief floods over me. "Do you want to eat something real quick before bed?"

She shakes her head. "No, I'd really just like to lie down."

Pumpkin, who disappeared when the commotion started, has reappeared and rubs his side up against Nana's leg.

"Well, who is this guy?" She smiles as she bends down to pet him. "His hair is almost the same hue as your father's."

"It is." I press my lips into a grin.

"I think we should keep him," she says.

"I agree." I stand and extend my hand toward my grandmother. This time, she takes it.

I walk with her toward her bedroom. "Where is your father, dear?"

"He's on his way," I respond, and she nods, satisfied.

I help her get into bed and tuck her in. "I want you to know I love you so much." My voice quivers.

"Oh, Evelyn. I love you, too, my darling."

"Stay with me as long as you can. Okay?" I plead, hugging her as I rest my cheek against her chest.

She pats my back. "I will stay with you forever and always, my dear."

I step out of my grandmother's room and close the door behind me. Hayes is in the kitchen, stirring a pitcher of liquid.

"What's that?" I ask him.

"Well, I thought maybe you'd want to take me up on the margarita after all?" he says in question.

I nod. "Um...yes, please."

He pours me a margarita and hands it to me before pouring himself one as well.

"What a mess." I sigh and take a drink. "The food's cold, you're surrounded by drama, and I'm a blubbering mess. I guess dinner alone in your hotel is sounding pretty enticing right about now."

"Evie," he says gently. "I'm so sorry about tonight. I'm sorry that you're going through this at all." He raises his hand and tucks a strand of hair behind my ear. "You're one of the strongest people I know."

"That can't be true." I chuckle dryly.

"It is." His deep brown eyes hold my stare.

"I guess we could warm everything up." I look at the dining room table full of untouched dishes.

"You know what I've always wanted to try?" he asks.

"What?"

"Cold tacos," he says, causing me to laugh.

"Stop it. You have not." I smile, and the act of it feels off, given the past few minutes, but I can't deny that it feels so much better than crying.

"No, seriously. In all of my life, I can't remember eating cold tacos. Cold pizza? Sure. Pasta right out of the refrigerator? Yep. Tacos? Never. I think it's time I rectify that situation."

I just shake my head and grin. "Okay." I shrug. "If that's what you really want."

"It definitely is."

We sit at the kitchen table and start plating up our

food. My drink went down quickly, and Hayes pours me another.

We drink margaritas and eat cold tacos.

Wanting the conversation to be on anything but Sweetie, me, and our sad situation, I ask, "So, you've been all over the United States? What is the craziest thing you've seen?"

Hayes tells me about a small town souvenir shop that he went to check out a couple of years back. The wife wanted to sell, but the store was in both her and her husband's names. She said that her husband ran off with an eighteen-year-old and skipped town. Regardless, Hayes couldn't buy the store without the husband present, so the deal fell through. Two months later, the husband's body was found in the basement in a large capacity freezer. The wife had found out about the husband's affair and killed him.

"Oh my gosh. That's crazy!" I say.

"Yeah." Hayes laughs. "I knew something was off about that woman during our meetings, but I would've never guessed that her dead husband was below us in the basement. I've definitely seen some crazy things out there. Believe it or not, all small towns are not as idealistic as Cherry Blossom Grove. Some of them are downright strange."

Hayes fixes himself another taco, "These are really good."

"You should try them warm," I kid.

"Nope. I like them this way." He looks at me and tilts his head. "Do you want to talk about it?"

"No, I don't. I actually want to do anything but." I take a sip of my drink. "Do you have any more stories?"

He nods. "I sure do."

I get lost in his words. His stories make me forget about the heaviness that surrounds me. I laugh at his tales, and I'm grateful because laughter is so much better than tears.

Chapter Nine

I pour coffee into my giant *Friends* mug. It's the largest mug I own, and I need the extra pick-me-up today.

That show was a favorite of ours growing up, and I've probably watched every episode ten times, at minimum. Pops loved Joey while Sweetie loved Phoebe. It's hard for me to pick a favorite as I love all of the characters, but I can't deny that most of the show's most iconic moments centered around Ross. His character was brilliant.

Wrapping my hands around the mug, I savor the first sip. It's always the best. Closing my eyes, I relish this moment of quiet and coffee before I start the day. *It's going to be a great day*, I tell myself. Yesterday turned into one of the worst, but today will be different.

Deep voices beyond our door, in the hallway, pull me from my thoughts.

I yank open the entry door to find Hayes with his fist raised, ready to knock. Mr. Kettleman, the local hardware store owner, stands to his side.

"Evie," Hayes addresses me with a startled expression. "You surprised me. Good morning."

"You surprised me, too. What are you doing here?" I question as I peek around him to see a windowpane held firmly in Mr. Kettleman's grasp.

"Good morning, dear," Mr. Kettleman says, his round face jolly as always. "I hear you're in need of a window fix?"

"How did you...but, you're not even open?" My questions blend, and I look at the clock on the kitchen wall. The hardware store doesn't open until nine, two hours from now.

"I know." Mr. Kettleman smiles, his cheeks red. "I was in the store this morning receiving a shipment, and the phone was ringing off the hook, so I finally picked up, and it was this nice gentleman here. He told me about the window, and I told him to come on over. Luckily, I had what you need in stock. Ms. Sweetie has been one of my dearest friends for almost sixty years. If she needs something, I'm here."

My heart melts at the kindness before me. "Thank you." My eyes well with tears, but I blink them away. "This way." I invite the men inside.

Mr. Kettleman leads the way with the glass in his grasp, and Hayes bends and grabs the toolbox and follows.

I grasp his arm as he passes. "Thank you so much," I tell him.

"It's nothing. Just a little small-town hospitality." He shoots me a wink and follows Mr. Kettleman into the living room.

Sweetie exits her bathroom, dressed and ready for the day to find the two men fixing her window.

"Frank?" she questions.

Mr. Kettleman turns and smiles, "Good morning, Ms. Sweetie."

"What are you doing here?" she asks.

"There was an accident with the window. Just fixing it for you," he says.

"Well, thank you. I wasn't aware it was broken." She looks at me in confusion.

"Just happened," I reassure her. "Mr. Kettleman wanted to get it fixed before you noticed."

My comment puts a smile on her face. "Well, of course, he does. That's our Frank, always looking out for everyone. Such a kind heart he has."

"Don't say that too loudly. Wouldn't want anyone to hear," Mr. Kettleman kids.

Sweetie swipes her hand through the air. "Oh, you. Always so humble." She turns and faces me. "Did I ever tell you about the first time your father and I met Frank?"

She had. "No," I respond.

"It was our first trip here...oh, about sixty years ago. Your father and I were heading out of town on a Sunday morning. We had spent all day Friday and Saturday here and had such a wonderful time. George needed to work on Monday morning, so we had to leave fairly early Sunday to get back home at a decent hour. Well, anyway...as we drove out of town, our car died. It just stopped working, smoke coming from under the hood. This young man stopped to see if we needed help. He was wearing a proper suit, dressed up all nice. We didn't know it at the time, but he was on his way to his niece's christening. But he didn't hesitate. Suit and all, he opened up the hood of the car and checked it out. Said we needed a part and that he'd be right back. Left us and came back thirty minutes later with the part and a tool-box. Fixed the car up and got us back on the road. Only took money from your father after he insisted. We found out later that he missed that christening to help us."

"Yeah, and I got quite the tongue-lashing from my father because of it," Mr. Kettleman says as he works on the window. "But, truth be told, I wasn't too sad to miss the church service. I've never felt comfortable in those stiff clothes. I'm much happier with tools in my hand."

"That sounds like something Mr. Kettleman would do." I grin.

"Oh, you ladies give me too much credit," he grumbles cheerfully.

Sweetie shakes her finger. "Oh, that is not true, and you know it. You're one of the good ones, Frank."

"As are you, Ms. Sweetie," he replies.

The guys finish up the window, and Nana helps me

in the kitchen. We don't have much to make them, but our offer of coffee, eggs, and toast is met with two enthusiastic yeses.

The four of us sit around the table, eating breakfast.

"I wish I had known you were coming. I would have made you some of my blueberry muffins," Sweetie tells Mr. Kettleman.

"Oh, you do make the best blueberry muffins. I will take a rain check on those, Ms. Sweetie."

I hold my coffee cup in my hands and take a sip. It's lukewarm at best, yet it's so much better than that cherished first sip. My grandmother is happy and talkative, and best of all, she remembers. Today is a good day.

I smile as Sweetie shares other stories about her past with Hayes, whom she thinks is Mr. Kettleman's new apprentice. She's always been a social butterfly. She knows everything there is to know about the residents of this town. She's everyone's friend and biggest supporter. She's been quieter over the past couple of months, so seeing her chatting our ears off this morning, especially after such a traumatic evening, is a true gift.

Eventually, we wrap up breakfast. Both Mr. Kettleman and I need to open up our businesses. Before he leaves, I retrieve my checkbook from my purse.

"What do I owe you?" I ask him.

"Nothing. It's taken care of."

"No. We are paying you for that window. I appreciate your generosity, and you've always been so wonderful to our family, but we are paying you. You have a business to run, too," I remind him.

He shakes his head and chuckles. "You remind me so much of her." His smile fades, and I know he's thinking about Sweetie and how fast she's leaving us. "But, as I was saying. It's been taken care of." He nods toward Hayes.

It's then I realize that Hayes has already paid. Why would he do that? He doesn't owe me this.

Mr. Kettleman picks up his toolbox and squeezes my forearm. "I'll see you around, Evie."

"Thanks again, Mr. Kettleman. I really appreciate it."

"Never hesitate to call me if you need something, day or night. I'm serious."

"Okay."

With a satisfied nod, he leaves.

Hayes follows him, stopping prior to leaving. "I'll see you in a few minutes, then?"

"How much do I owe you for the window? You don't need to pay for it. Sweetie and I can take care of ourselves, Hayes. It's a nice gesture but not needed. Let me pay you back."

"That won't be necessary," he says.

"Hayes," I warn. "I'm paying for the window."

He tilts his head to the side, his eyes squinting. "You know, for someone who likes to dish out kindness like confetti, you really need to work on accepting it in return."

I pull in a breath. "It was very nice, and I appreciate it. Truly, I do. But it's not your job to take care of us. It's my job, and I can do it. You're here to learn about the business and move on. You're not here to take care of us. Plus, it's not good for business."

"It's not good for business?" Hayes quirks a brow.

"Yeah, I mean, you're the buyer, and I'm the seller. We are completing a business transaction. We could muddy everything up with you paying to fix something in my apartment that's not your responsibility. You know?"

"No, I don't," he answers simply.

"Please let me pay for it," I plead.

"That's very nice, and I appreciate it. Truly, I do. But it's not your job to decide what I can spend my money on. It's not good for business." He echoes my words from moments ago with a smirk on his face. "Seriously, just say thank you and let it go. I wanted to help. Just let me be nice. Okay?" He chuckles.

"Okay." I sigh, my lips turning up in a grin. "Thank you."

"Why, you're welcome. I'll see you downstairs. Thank you for breakfast," he says before turning to leave.

I shut the door behind him and lean against it.

An annoying high-pitched meow sounds at my feet.

I sigh. "Well, thank you for waiting until our guests left," I tell Pumpkin. "That was very generous of you."

Pumpkin releases a long, whiny meow, which, if I

had to translate, would mean, "Yes, it was. Now hurry up with my food, human."

I open a can of food for Pumpkin and scrape it into his dish. "There you go, your highness."

In the living room, I find Nana looking out our new window.

"I'm going to head down to the shop. Would you like to come along for a little bit? Hester is stopping by with some ice cream for the floats."

Hester is another friend of hers and Pops' from the beginning of their time here, so I think she'll remember him. She seems to hold on to distant memories.

"A fresh root beer float would be nice. For some reason, I feel as if I haven't had one in a very long time. Have I?" She turns to me, panic starting to line her features.

"I haven't either," I reassure her. "We've just been so busy with the cherry season and all the new visitors arriving. You know the cherry festival kicks off tomorrow. If you're up to it, you can join me."

"Oh, I do love the cherry festival."

"Me too, Sweetie."

Chapter Ten

Evie - 18 Years Old

"This is the perfect color dress for you," Abby says as she takes my hand and twirls me around. "You should wear emerald green at all times."

"Okay, I'll work on that." I laugh.

"Seriously, the way it complements your eyes and looks next to your hair. It's seriously stunning. Eli is going to die when he sees you," Abby calls out to Hazel. "Eli's going to flip. Right, Hazel?"

"Definitely," Hazel agrees as she pins up a curled strand of her ebony locks.

"It doesn't matter anyway," I tell them both. "I got the dress because I love it, not to impress anyone. I told you that Eli and I are going to prom as friends. Nothing more."

"I don't buy it," Abby says. "I know he's smitten."

I walk over to my dresser and grab my lip gloss, then peer over Hazel's shoulder into the mirror. "Even if he is, it doesn't mean that I am." I apply the shiny tint to my lips. "Not every relationship is fairy-tale love, Abby. Just because you and Beckett started dating when you were five doesn't mean that all other couplings carry the same perfection."

"Excuse me." She scoffs with mock annoyance. "We were best friends since we were five but didn't start dating until I was like thirteen."

Hazel wraps the curling iron around another strand of hair. "Yeah, it's hard for you to give relationship advice, Abby, because your reality is so different from the norm."

"It's not that different. I'm sure lots of people marry their childhood sweethearts. Right?" Abby pulls a pale pink strapless princess dress with a huge tulle skirt from a garment bag. "Can you help me get into this?" she asks me.

"Sure, this dress is amazing. It's so much more your style than that tight black one you almost got," I say to Abby, holding her dress out in front of me. She grabs my shoulders, steadying herself, and steps in.

"And Abby," Hazel says, "I'm pretty sure like less than one percent of people marry their childhood sweetheart. It's definitely far from common."

"It's more than one percent. I'm sure of it," Abby protests. She turns around and holds her long blonde hair that's been curled into ringlets to the side as I zip her up. "Are you almost done?" she asks Hazel. "I need you to pin up my hair."

"Yep. Almost finished. One sec." Hazel holds a mirror up and turns around so she can see the back of her hair.

"It looks great," I assure her.

The three of us have started this tradition of getting ready for formal events in my room. Preparation for homecoming, prom, and any other dances usually starts here. It started out of convenience since my apartment is in town and Hazel and Abby live a ways out. Then a handful of our friends, including Eli, live on the opposite side of town. The shop is pretty central to our friend group and close to the school. Plus, Pops and Sweetie always make it special with mocktails and treats down in the shop for a little pre-party.

"Do you really think you and Beckett will get married someday?" I ask Abby. I guess I've always assumed they would, but then again, it is rare for someone to just have one love in their lifetime.

Abby doesn't hesitate. "I really do, a hundred percent. Not a doubt in my mind."

"We brought drinks, and no doubt about what?" Sweetie asks from the doorway. She and Pops stand there holding fruit punch drinks in martini glasses.

Pops steps into my room and hands us each a drink.

Abby speaks up, "I was just telling them that I think Beckett and I are going to get married someday."

"Oh, I believe that," Pops chimes in, and we all look at him.

"Really?" I ask him.

"Of course. I told you girls about Sweetie and me, right?" he says to Hazel and Abby.

I've heard the story many times, but it always makes me smile when he retells it.

"Why don't you tell us?" Abby says, now sitting before Hazel as she works her magic on Abby's hair.

Pops stands up straight and clears his throat. "Well, I met this sassy little auburn-haired girl when we were in the third grade. She wore her hair in the same style every day, two long braids with small blue bows. I found her incredibly interesting. She was so different from me. She was serious and studious and smart." He looks at Sweetie with so much love.

"You see, I was the youngest of seven boys. We lived on a farm, and I'd been up for hours doing chores before school started. Most of the time, I was running into school ten minutes late, shirt untucked, tripping over hand-me-down pants that were too big. Once I even wore mismatched shoes. I had my older brother Gary's boot on my left foot and my brown dress shoe on my right. I didn't even notice until I got to school, and someone pointed it out. Gary was not happy with me that day." Pops chuckles. "The truth was, school wasn't very interesting to me. So, while the love of my life here took it very seriously, I did not. I was quite the prankster of our class."

Sweetie laughs under her breath and shakes her head.

"Is something funny, dear?" Pops asks her.

"Just remembering you back then. You were something else." She chuckles.

"I was," he agrees and turns his attention back to us girls. "You see, I made it my mission to flirt with Sweetie, but what I thought was flirting, she thought was bullying."

"You put a spider in my hair," she deadpans.

"It was funny," he retorts.

"It was mean." She puckers her lips.

"Well, I didn't mean for it to be mean. I didn't have any sisters, and my brothers and I were always pulling pranks on one another. I was young. I just knew that I had to get little Miss Edith to notice me. So, one day after class, I pulled the blue bow out of her hair, and she turned on me and yelled, 'George Emberton, I am going to tell your mother!' I remember my eyes going wide, and I said, 'You're sassy.' She huffed, and said, 'I am not. I'm sweet as pie, but you're mean.' Then she grabbed the bow from my hand and stormed off. I knew then she was the one for me. So, the next day, I brought her a lollipop and love note."

Sweetie smiles. "He sure did. He was quite the little romantic for a nine-year-old."

"From that day on, Sweetie was the only girl who garnered my attention. Age isn't of importance. When you know, you know. I felt it in here." He holds his hand to his heart. "She had my heart, and once someone truly holds your heart, there's no one else. She was my first and only love, and I wouldn't want it any other way."

"Aw." The girls sigh.

"So, if Beckett holds your heart, Abby, then I believe he'll be your forever," Pops says.

"You are such a romantic," Hazel says to Pops.

"Well, it's easy to be when I met my one and only at nine years old." He puts his arm around Sweetie and pulls her into a kiss.

"Okay. Okay. We'll be out of here in a few," I tease.

Sweetie pulls away from the kiss. "Oh, yes. Speaking of that. Beckett, Callan, Eli, and Matty and his date are downstairs in the shop."

"Perfect because I'm finished," Hazel says as she sprays Abby's hair.

"So, what's the plan?" Pops asks.

"We'll hang out downstairs for a little bit and get some pictures. Then Hazel's parents have the horse-drawn carriage arriving at six to pick us up. The carriage will take us to the B&B, where we'll get more pictures and meet up with Aubrey and her date. Aubrey's parents have the fancy dining room set up for us, and Matty's parents are catering dinner. Then the carriage is taking us to the dance," I tell them.

"So we'll follow the carriage in the car to take pictures at Aubrey's," Sweetie adds.

"Perfect." I nod.

"Everything is so fancy nowadays," Pops says to Sweetie. "Do you remember our prom?"

Sweetie chuckles. "A story for another day, dear. Let the girls finish getting ready." She playfully pushes Pops toward the door. "We'll head downstairs so we can get photos of you three walking down the stairs. You all look like princesses, just darling," she says before following Pops out of my room.

"Your grandparents are the cutest." Hazel sighs. "I don't know if I'm ever going to find my one true love, the one who owns my heart or whatever your pops just said."

"Ditto," I say. "No boy has come close to holding my heart."

"Well, then give Eli a chance." Abby scoffs. "You're never going to find love if you don't open your heart up to it."

"Fine. I'll try, but honestly, I don't think my heart holder goes to our high school." I giggle.

"Same." Hazel laughs with me. "Regardless, though, we are going to be the hottest girls in Cherry Blossom Grove tonight."

"Obviously," Abby agrees.

All dolled up, my two best friends and I start for the shop where the evening of our senior prom is set to begin. I'll keep my word to Abby and try to see Eli as more than a friend. I've heard many renditions of my grandparents' courtship from nine years old to marriage at nineteen, and each story is sweeter than the last. I want to hold out for that kind of love. I feel that true love, like my grandparents share, will come easily, and it won't be forced. It will happen despite any obstacles, and it'll be right, and forever.

Chapter Eleven

Our teal and pink candy-printed canopy tent stands upright outside the front door of Sweet as Pie. Beneath the tent rests a table full of treats. There's a large selection of free candies that everyone of all ages will enjoy, and there's also pre-bagged goodies for sale. Beside the table is the letter board sign reminding all that everyone is welcome to a free small root beer float.

I carried down Sweetie's comfortable cushioned chair from the apartment for her to sit in. She's always loved Cherry Festival day. Every business on our main street is out on the sidewalk with tents and items on display. Musicians come from all over Michigan to play on the street corners for the crowds. Outside of Amigos is a street taco stand that's always a crowd favorite. Today, an award-winning chalk artist from Ann Arbor, Michigan, came to draw chalk art with the crowds.

Cherry Festival is a giant street party, and it's amazing. I've been to more cherry festivals than I can count, and I still feel the magic of each and every one.

"So, this is the cherry festival? Pretty cool," Hayes says from beside me.

"It's more than cool." I scoff. "It's incredible."

He laughs. "It is. I agree. But I'm confused because I saw that there is another cherry festival next Thursday?"

"Yeah, so this is the main cherry festival, and it lasts for four days—today, Friday, Saturday, and Sunday. It's the kickoff to cherry season and a serious four-day party. Then every Thursday throughout the rest of the summer is also called cherry festival, but those are just one day each week."

"So, this cherry festival is a four-day festival, but the other cherry festivals are just one day, on Thursdays throughout the summer?" Hayes clarifies.

"Exactly. Except for the other four-day one right in the middle of picking season at the end of July. This one gets everyone excited for the upcoming season, and the other four-day one celebrates the picking season. Then the Thursday ones are just to celebrate, period."

"Well, that's not confusing at all." He chuckles.

"It's really not. Everyone gets it." I eye him accusingly. "Well, almost everyone."

"I just think that it wouldn't have hurt to call the kickoff party one name and the Thursday parties another, and the mid-season one another."

I shrug. "Well, considering they are all cherry festivals, it only made sense to do it this way. Look, Mister," I tease. "We are set in our ways here in Cherry Blossom Grove. Don't come here with your New Yorker ideas and try to change things up. Isn't the purpose of your month here to learn the native CBG ways?" I raise a brow.

"And clearly, I need the whole month. Let me guess. You have black Friday sales on the day after Thanksgiving but also on every other Monday?" He puckers his lips.

I smack him playfully with a laugh. "Stop. Now, that obviously wouldn't make any sense."

Hayes looks back toward Sweetie. "I wasn't aware that he's an outdoor cat." He gestures to Pumpkin, who rests on Sweetie's lap.

"He's not."

"Aren't you afraid of him running off?"

I huff out a laugh. "Are you kidding? He'd never leave. He's too dependent on the posh life he has going here. He's no dummy. He knows that there are not two cans of gourmet wet food a day anywhere out there but here."

Hayes shakes his head with a grin. "Okay. Just making sure. Your nana seems very fond of him."

I turn to see Sweetie gently petting Pumpkin across her lap. She wears a serene smile as she looks out to all of the people walking by, and it makes me so happy.

"No, he's good. He'd never leave," I say again, more to myself than Hayes. Pumpkin may be a lot of things, and most of them would be considered faults, but I could never fault him for the way he loves her.

"Evie!" A familiar voice pulls me from my thoughts.

I snap my face forward and clap my hands. "Eli! How are you?"

"Good. Just came by for a root beer float, of course."

"Absolutely," I say before addressing Hayes. "Keep an eye on things out here?"

"Sure," Hayes answers.

"Great. Come on in, Eli." I lead my friend into the shop. "So, how are things?"

He hands me the largest cup we carry, and I start to fill it with ice cream. "Real good. Just keeping busy on the farm. You know how it is."

The farm that supplies our ice cream belongs to Eli's father, and grandfather before him.

"I do but actually not for much longer," I say.

"I heard. That's what the suit is doing out there." He nods toward the sidewalk where Hayes stands.

The fact that he called him "the suit" makes me giggle. It's true that Hayes is still very much the businessman from New York. Anyone who sees him knows he isn't a Cherry Blossom Grove resident.

"Yeah. He's really nice despite how stiff he may look. I appreciate that he wants to see how we run the business. Keeping the same culture of the shop is important to him, which makes me feel less nervous about selling," I say as I pour the root beer into the cup.

"That's good, I guess. It's just going to be so weird

having some out of town company own Sweet as Pie." He frowns.

I blow out a sigh. "I know. Believe me. I've thought this over a lot, and it's just something I need to do."

He shakes his head. "I'm sorry. I shouldn't have made you feel bad. That wasn't my intention. I feel horrible about everything you're going through, Evie. Really I do."

I squeeze his hand. "Thank you, Eli. That means a lot." I hand him the float, and he hands me a five-dollar bill.

"Don't even argue with me. Put the money in the cash register."

I laugh at his firm tone and do what I'm told.

"So, how is Sweetie doing?" he asks and takes a sip.

I update my friend on the latest happenings. We both work so much, as do most of my friends, so I cherish these times when I can chat with those closest to me. A number of my friends work for their family businesses. Many occupations have hard workers, I know that, but there is something about working for oneself that pushes one to work even harder.

We catch up for a few more minutes. Eli updated me on what's going on with his family before Hayes and a handful of teen girls come into the shop.

"We need ten of the complimentary root beer floats for this group. Sasha here is celebrating her thirteenth birthday," Hayes says.

Eli whispers a quick goodbye and heads out.

"Happy Birthday!" I say to the girl who Hayes pointed out. "Cherry festival is a wonderful place to celebrate. Ten root beer floats coming up!"

I grab our small cup and the birthday girl protests. "Can I have the big one, please?"

Looking toward the man standing behind the group of girls, who I can only assume is the birthday girl's dad, I raise an eyebrow in question.

"Give them all the big one," he tells me. "Our neighbors have been raving about these floats since they came here last summer. It's one of the main reasons Hailey wanted to celebrate her birthday here."

"Well, your neighbors are correct. We have the best floats ever. The ice cream is made by a local farmer and is so creamy. You're going to love it," I say to the girls.

I chat with the teens as I hand out their dessert drinks and take the man's payment as the girls dance their way out of the shop, root beer floats in hand.

"You're so good with people," Hayes tells me after the group has left.

"How's it going outside?" I ask him.

"Good. Busy. Sweetie is getting lots of visitors. I think she's having fun."

"Yeah, she loves Cherry Festival." I grin.

"Which cherry festival, the four-day or the Thursday?" His stare holds mine and keeps a serious face for a second before his smile breaks.

I open my eyes wide and lean toward him. "All of them."

"Why do you give your root beer floats away for free? Doesn't seem like a good business move," he wonders as we walk back outside.

"We've already talked about this." I chuckle. "It's a good human move and a good business move."

"How is giving things away for free a good business move?" He lowers his gaze.

"Do you know how many free floats I've given away today?"

"How many?"

"Zero," I say slowly. "Most people upgrade their complimentary float to a bigger size and pay. For those who've never tried them, it's a risk-free way to do so, and chances are, they'll love it and buy one next time. And for those who truly can't afford one, it gives them the chance to have one anyway. I told you, everything works out."

Hayes bites his bottom lip and nods. "Okay, you may have a point."

"I do." I laugh.

"Who was that guy you were in there talking with?" he asks as I hand out handmade lollipops to some of the kids passing by.

"That was Eli. His family runs the dairy where we get our ice cream. He's been my friend for years. We graduated together. We actually went to senior prom together. He's a good guy."

"So, he's your ex?"

I tilt my head, contemplating. "Yeah, I guess so. We

weren't really serious in high school, more friends than anything. But he is the last person I've gone on a date with."

"Your last date was in high school?"

"Hey." I swat Hayes's arm. "Don't judge. I've been busy."

His eyebrows squish together. "I'm not judging. I'm just surprised. That's a long time ago, Evie."

I roll my eyes. "Believe me, I know."

"How much do you date Mr. Travel-Around-Constantly-Guy?" I huff out.

His lip tilts up. "Travel-Around-Constantly-Guy?" he questions.

Elbows bent and palms up, I shrug. "It's all I could think of on short notice," I quip.

He chuckles. "Well, not a lot, but I've been on quite a few dates since high school."

I shake my head. "Truthfully, the past seven years have been a blur. I don't know where the time has gone. I've worked a lot and helped my grandmother." I turn back to see Sweetie. She's chatting with a little boy. He's asking questions about Pumpkin and petting his orange fur. "But it's been worth it. You know I don't even remember my parents, and I lost my Pops way too soon. She's all I have left. I would do anything for her and not regret a second of it. At the end of the day, it's the people in your life who matter. Nothing else does. I have amazing friends, an incredible community, and a Nana who loves me. She may not remember me most days, but she loves me."

"She would want you to find someone and build a life, you know?" Hayes says.

"I know, and I will when the time is right. That's why I'm selling the shop. To start my life and my new business. Baby steps. Right?"

Hayes nods.

"Are you here to learn about the business or play relationship counselor?" I tease.

"Evidently, I'm here to learn how to give away all profitable goods for free." He eyes the little boy who was just talking to Sweetie as he reaches his small hands into the bin of free wrapped candies and pulls out two heaping handfuls.

The grimace on Hayes' face is hysterical, and I throw my head back in laughter.

"Let me guess?" he questions. "It all works out?"

"Yep." I enunciate the 'p' sound, letting it pop off my lips, then shrug with a smirk. "It all works out."

Chapter Twelve

I flip over the open sign on the storefront window and unlock the door. The street outside is still relatively quiet. Many of the tourists we get like to sleep in, so the mornings aren't as busy as the rest of the day.

Walking to the back counter, I wipe all of the glass candy cases with a dry cotton rag, ensuring to wipe clean any signs of dust or fingerprints. I scrub the whole store every night, but the morning sun shining through the window always helps me find fingerprints I may have missed.

"Evie!" Hayes shouts my name as he enters the shop, causing me to jump.

I hold my hand to my chest. "Oh, my goodness, Hayes. Why are you yelling?" I laugh.

"Because I have some exciting news for you." He grins wide.

"Oh, yeah?" I toss the cotton cloth behind the counter.

"So, I've been thinking a lot about how our philosophies about business are so varied. You like to give stuff away while I like to make money," he jokes. "You're always telling me about this small-town culture that you've grown up with, and though I see a lot of it working here with you, I realized that I'm missing out on a lot staying at the hotel where I'm secluded in my room. So, I checked out of the hotel and into Cherry Blossom Bed and Breakfast."

"Ooh!" I clap. "You're staying at Audrey's place?"

"Let me guess, Audrey Laurent is your close friend?" He questions with a dismissive stare.

"Yes, we went to school together."

"Of course you did." He shakes his head.

"She doesn't own the B&B yet. Her parents do, but she'll take over someday," I clarify.

"Of course she will," Hayes deadpans. "Anyway, so I'm staying at the B&B now because I figure I'll get to talk to a lot of people, get to hear firsthand from tourists about why they come, talk with local vendors who deliver to the B&B, eat meals with them...immerse myself in the local culture, if you will." He smirks, pleased with himself.

"That's great!"

He smiles. "I knew you'd approve. This morning, over a delicious meal of biscuits and gravy and cherry breakfast cake, I sat across from this couple who is here to scope out the area for their wedding next year. They just got engaged and are here to put deposits down on the venue and services for next summer. I told them about the local photographer, and they would love to get engagement shots taken. They have a tight schedule but have from two to four available today. Their names are Jen and Ed, and I told them that you'd meet them in the lobby at the B&B at two."

"What?" I gasp.

"Surprise!"

"Hayes, no." I shake my head. "I'm not ready for that. I can't...I have..." I stumble on my words.

"I've seen your shots, Evie. You're good. You have a talent with the camera, and you know what you're doing. You're ready. Plus, this will be great practice, and the shots will help you build your portfolio. And if they love the shots, they'll probably hire you as their wedding photographer next summer. Don't charge them if it makes you feel better. Say that you're using the photos for your website so they are free of charge. But do this. It will be great."

"I do need to build my portfolio." I sigh. "There are some great places I could take them to get beautiful shots." I think out loud. "I can do this."

"Of course you can," Hayes agrees.

"Okay!" I bounce up on my toes. "Thank you so much," I say before wrapping my arms around Hayes. "That was so nice of you."

"It was nothing." He hugs me back.

My arms fall, and I look into his eyes. "No, it's definitely not nothing, Hayes." I place my open palm against my chest. "Thank you."

He swallows. "You're welcome. I will chat you up over breakfast anytime." He supplies a wink. "I was thinking that after we do any shop stuff that needs to be done, you can sign me into your website, and I'll work on updating that for you while you're gone. Then when you come back with all of the incredible shots you took, we can upload the best ones onto your online portfolio."

"That would be amazing! Let me go get my stuff."

I jog up the steps toward the apartment.

Christine, the nurse that I hired to stay with Nana while I'm working, is hand washing dishes in the kitchen when I enter.

"Christine, you don't have to do our dishes. I can wash them when I get back tonight." I eye the sink full of sudsy water. "And, you know we have a dishwasher."

"Oh, I like washing dishes. My family says I'm crazy, but I've always found it soothing, the warm water, the bubbles, the calming motion of scrubbing the dishes. I just like it." she shrugs. "Plus, your Sweetie's just watching her shows. At least I can make myself a little helpful."

"You're very helpful. It takes a huge weight off my shoulders that you're here with her during the day. I don't have to worry that she's scared or confused."

"I'm glad to do it. She's a wonderfully kind woman," Christine says.

"Yes, she is." I smile warmly. "Anyway, I just have to grab a few things, and I'll be heading back downstairs."

I find my laptop, charger, and camera bag in my room. I grab them and make my way back downstairs. Hayes is checking out a local customer, and I stand back and watch. Besides the suits he wears all of the time, he really does fit in here. He may be a city boy, but he has the small-town charm.

"I look forward to it, Mrs. Ackerman. You have a great day," he says as Mrs. Ackerman takes her paper bag of goodies and leaves the shop.

"What are you looking forward to?" I ask, setting my laptop and camera bag on the counter.

"Well, turns out that she makes the best fried chicken in the land." He quirks an eyebrow. "And apparently, no matter how many times she offered it to you and your grandparents, you declined. So, she is delighted I have accepted her offer of a fried chicken dinner."

I chuckle. "We declined because we're vegetarians, and we told her that." I shake my head. "I'm telling you, eating meat is a religion to some people. Some individuals really can't understand why anyone would choose not to." A memory comes to mind. "Once she brought us this vegetable soup...oh, I should tell you, sharing food is also a big deal in small-town culture. So, anyway...she brought us this vegetable soup because 'she knew we liked vegetables.' Looking at the soup, you could see huge chunks of bacon in it, and I told her sure, many people in town would love her soup and that I was positive it was delicious, but we simply didn't eat bacon. And do you know what she said?"

"What?" Hayes asks eagerly.

"She said, 'If you eat bacon, are you going to die?' and I politely told her that no, I wouldn't die, but I don't want to eat it. Gotta love her." I huff out a laugh. "She means well."

"I get it. Bacon was considered a food group for my grandpa. I swear he ate it at every meal. Some people have a hard time seeing the world through lenses other than their own."

"That's true. I don't take it to heart, though. Mrs. Ackerman is a wonderful person and does a lot for people in the community. And her fried chicken is legendary around these parts, so I'm sure you'll love it."

"She definitely loves it, the way she went on about it, and you know what else she loves? Chocolate-covered cashews—she bought almost thirty dollars worth of the things."

"Oh yeah, she loves her chocolate-covered cashews. Comes in every week for them."

Hayes looks toward my laptop. "Should we get started?"

"Might as well. I can pull up the website information for you. While you go through that, I'm going to make sure my camera batteries are charged, and my settings and memory card are ready."

"Cool. Where are you going to take them?" Hayes

asks. I pull up my website and slide the laptop toward him.

I start going through my camera supplies. "There are a lot of beautiful places on the grounds of the bed and breakfast—wooded areas, a stream, and a grassy hill that should still have its early summer wildflowers."

"Yeah, the grounds there are beautiful as is the bed and breakfast itself. It reminds me of some of the older homes in the Hamptons, very Old English cottage, Cape Cod feel to it."

"Yeah, Audrey's grandparents came over from France, and on their journey, her grandmother fell in love with both styles of those homes. She incorporated all of her favorite parts of the houses they passed in their travels into the design of the B&B. It's definitely one of the most beautiful structures in Cherry Blossom Grove, if not the most beautiful. I love it there."

I put a new memory card into the camera and check to make sure it's blank and ready to hold lots of pictures. "The orchards are beautiful right now as well. New cherries are on the trees. I could get some incredible shots there as well."

"I bet you could. Plus, the orchards are kind of the entire reason for this whole town, right?"

"You could say that." I chuckle.

"You should definitely take them there. They'd love it." Hayes clicks away on my laptop.

"Who else is staying at the bed and breakfast? Anyone celebrating a birthday or anniversary? Anyone with pets? A family reunion?" I start to get excited at the possibilities to build my portfolio and experience.

"Well, at breakfast, it was Jen and Ed and me for a while. As I was finishing up, an older couple came down to eat. Maybe they're here celebrating an anniversary? I'll talk to them tonight." He shoots me a wink.

"Thank you." I laugh. "It will be fun to have my own inside man, scoping out the clientele."

"At your service."

One of the main reasons for selling the shop was to start my career as a photographer, but it seems surreal that my first photoshoot is today. Hayes gave me the push I needed.

"Christine is leaving at four today," I say to myself more than anyone as I realize that might present a problem.

"If you're not back, I'll go upstairs and sit with Sweetie until you get back. I haven't had a *Golden Girls* fix in a few days, so I'm due," he volunteers before I can even think to ask him. My chest swells with gratitude for Hayes and everything he's done for me since he's arrived.

"Thank you so much," I say.

"Don't mention it. It will be fun. I could even put a roast or, in your case, some carrots in the oven while you're gone," he says, causing me to laugh.

Our relationship revolves around business, but I can't pretend that I'm not starting to really like having him here. I know he's here to get the scoop on my business to make it successful after the sale, but that doesn't include helping me with my new career, getting to know the locals, fixing my window, or helping me with Nana. Yet he does it all anyway.

He's becoming part of life here in Cherry Blossom Grove, yet his time here is fleeting. He'll be gone soon, and I'll miss him. I know I shouldn't, but I will.

Chapter Thirteen

Hayes and I sit side by side at the counter, each staring at a laptop. He works on projects for his company that I can only assume entail buying out quaint stores from one small town to the next. While I work on editing photos from yesterday's photoshoot.

"What do you think of this one?" I ask, turning my screen toward him.

When Hayes leans over to look, I inhale on instinct. He always smells the same—a mixture of clean, pine, and musk. It's intoxicating, though I pretend it's not.

"Oh, I love that one." He stares at the picture of the three-year-old girl on my screen. He met her and her parents at the bed and breakfast and convinced them to have birthday pictures done. I should feel a little guilty that he's obtaining all these clients for me over a seemingly innocent bowl of oatmeal, but when I look at the moments I'm capturing of these families, I'm proud of these memories they'll have forever. "I love the lighting in this one, how it comes through the leaves and the way you blurred the background, making her the focal point. It's a stunning photo, Evie."

I'm incredibly proud of this shot too, but it feels good to hear it from someone else. "Thanks."

"I'll definitely be putting that one on the website," he says.

Thanks to Hayes, my website is updated and more professional looking than it's ever been.

Hazel walks through the front door holding two bottles of wine. "Hello. Hello. Hello. Are we ready for the parade?"

"Hey, you." I get up from my chair and walk around the counter to give her a hug.

"These are for you." She hands me the bottles of wine. "And your float is parked right behind ours, lined up and ready to go."

"Thank you! You're the best."

"All right. Well, I'm going to head out. See you in a bit!"

"We'll be there in a couple of minutes," I tell her.

It's almost time for the annual cherry parade. Hazel's family stores our float in one of their barns and brings it to us every year for the parade.

"Let me go check on Sweetie and remind the nurse to have her down by the road in a few minutes to watch the parade. I'll be right back," I tell Hayes before jogging up the stairs to the apartment.

When I return, he's put our laptops away and is ready to go.

I grab the two large bags of candy, and we step outside. Hayes takes the bags from me, and I lock up the shop. "Tell me about this parade again. It's to celebrate the start of cherry-picking season?"

"Yes." I nod.

"But the cherries aren't ready to pick yet?"

"Correct. It's still a week or so early."

"Yet you're having the parade now, so it won't be too close to the 4th of July?"

"Yep. Because there's another parade then for the holiday. We need to spread them out a little."

"Right..." Hayes drags out. "Makes sense." He grins.

"One thing you need to know about small towns is that we love parades. We have them for all of the holidays, one at the beginning of cherry season and one at the end, and one at the beginning of fair week and one at the end of fair week."

"Fair, like animals?"

"Yeah, animals, 4-H, crafts, food, games, rides...all that jazz."

Hayes laughs. "You guys love to celebrate."

"Of course. It's fun."

"You have a booth at the fair, don't you?" he inquires.

"Obviously." I shoot him a wink.

"And when is that?"

"The fair is in August," I tell him just as we walk up to our float. "Ta-da." I extend my palm down the float Vanna White style. Our float is decades old, but my pops put so much care into making it that it's held up well. It's hot pink and white striped with a giant lollipop at each corner. Between each human-sized lollipop are garlands of plastic candies. In the center of the float is a pink throne made of faux licorice and across from the throne at the end of the float is a four-foot-tall root beer float.

"Nice." Hayes grins. "Did your grandfather make this?"

"He did. It's almost twenty years old, but he did such a great job constructing it that it's held up well." I run my hand along the outside of the float. "I guess, I'll be giving this to whoever takes over the shop. They'll need it." I whip my head toward Hayes. "This is my last parade." That reality just dawned on me. "I've been in every parade since I was born." My voice drops. "Gosh, that makes me sad."

"I'm sure you can still be a part of the parade if you want. I guarantee the new manager of the shop will welcome your help."

"Yeah." I pause, turning a wrapped candy from the garland between my fingers. "It won't be the same, though, because it won't be mine."

"Oh, wait," I say, snapping out of my funk. "I forgot. I sign over the business after the 4th of July. So, I still have one more. Phew. I'll save my melancholy for that one."

"Sounds good."

The bell sounds, indicating the parade starts in five minutes.

"Okay, I'll take these." I retrieve the bags of candy from Hayes and put them on the float. "You're confident you can drive the truck? If not, you can throw the candy and wave, and I'll drive."

Hayes chuckles. "I can drive."

"Okay, you'll just follow Hazel's float in front of you. Just keep some distance, and go slow."

"Got it," he reassures me and grabs my hand, helping me onto the float. Once I'm on the float, he asks, "If you give out candy, does that mean Hazel hands out wine bottles?" he teases.

"Yeah," I answer, and his smile drops.

"Really?"

"Well, mini ones and only to the adults. She gives out grape-flavored suckers to the kids. If places can give out samples of what they sell, they usually do. Obviously, not everyone can. Like the funeral home hands out Frisbees with their logo."

"Well, that's good. I'd hate to think what else they could share." He shivers, and I laugh.

"Have fun," he tells me.

"You too."

* * *

The parade was a blast, as they all are. I love looking at the kids' faces as I toss them candy. Nothing is better than the pure joy looking back at me. The beginning of cherry season parade is one of my favorites. Since cherry picking hasn't officially started, fewer tourists are present than at the parades later in the summer. I love the tourists, too, of course. But it's fun looking down from my float made of candy at the faces I've known all of my life or, in the case of the children, their lives.

The young and the old line Main Street in their chairs to wave at the parade. It's such a celebration of joy and community. I suppose after the Independence Day parade, I'll get to experience it from a spectator's point of view. I've never seen it that way before. It could be good.

"That was great," Hayes tells me as we walk back to the apartment.

"I'm glad you had fun. I think being on the float is a little more exciting than driving, but at least you got the gist of the event."

"Yeah, I loved it."

"Are you typing up the parade into your corporate plan for the shop once the sale is final?" I ask, still confused as to what he's even doing here. I understand his thought process and wanting to make sure the shop is successful after he leaves, but a month seems like an awfully long time. Honestly, he's done more to help Sweetie and me than I've done for him. I'm just not sure what "brilliance" he's collecting that will help him or anyone else run the shop.

"Definitely. These town-wide events are great for advertising. Plus, I think at this point, if the shop didn't participate, there'd be a riot of little children at the front door demanding candy."

"That's probably true." I smile at the image. "They've come to expect some candy at these parades." I tilt my head up to Hayes. "I want to thank you for everything you've done for Sweetie and me since you've been here. I hope I've helped you prepare your plan for the shop because I feel like you've been more helpful to us. Like I should be doing more or giving you more information somehow."

Hayes waves a hand dismissively in the air. "Not at all. You've been great, and I've learned a lot about this small-town life you love so much. You know, I travel around and buy these businesses, overhaul them, and set them up with new management that reports to my company, yet I've never really stayed in one place long enough to truly understand why these small communities work so well. This experience has been eye-opening for me. Of course, I've known that small-town life is vastly different than big city life, but staying here has helped me appreciate what that means. It's been great. Honestly. I'll look at future purchases in different towns with a new lens, and I know that'll only help."

I nod, content with his answer. "Good. I'm glad I could teach you so much," I tease. "I've realized that you know so much about me, but I don't know a lot about you."

"What do you want to know?"

"All of it. What's your family like. Where'd you grow up? Anything really."

We walk past the door of the shop and continue down Main Street. It's a beautiful summer night, and I don't think either of us is ready to call it a night just yet.

"I grew up with a great family about two hours north of New York City. It's considered a smaller town, but it's still a lot bigger than here. My parents are high school sweethearts and are still as much in love with each other today as they were in high school. I have a twin sister named Hattie."

I cut in. "Oh my gosh, you're a twin?"

"I am." he smiles. "She's the best person I know. The two of you would get along great. We also have a sister six years younger than us. Her name is Grace."

We pass the local bakery and stop to look at the treats in the window. There's a tray of cupcakes with frosted cherries on top of each one. What looks like a three-tiered wedding cake is on display beside the cupcakes. The cake has cascading frosting cherries that start at the top and wind their way down each layer.

"I've been to many small towns, and I will say that yours is more consistently themed than any other place I've been to. You people seriously worship the cherry." He laughs.

I shrug. "Yeah, well, this town wouldn't exist without it." I eye the cupcakes. "This bakery is family-owned as well. I'm friends with the son of the owners."

"Of course you are." Hayes chuckles.

"I'm just glad I grew up in a candy shop and not a bakery. Cupcakes are my weakness. If I owned this place, you'd probably have to roll me down this sidewalk right now."

"I doubt that. Their novelty would wear off some. You grew up surrounded by a hundred varieties of sweet treats, and you're just perfect."

The way he calls me perfect does something funny to my insides. I rub my arms, feeling a heat followed by a shiver traveling over my skin.

I clear my throat and step away from the bakery. "So, friends? Do you have a lot of friends back home?"

"A few. Not as many as you." He grins. "You might not believe this, but I was quite serious as a child."

"Oh, I can totally see that." I laugh.

"I was a little bit of a perfectionist. I liked to be the best at whatever I did, and I worked really hard, especially on my studies. I went above and beyond in all classes, determined to graduate at the top of my class."

"And did you?"

"I did. I went to Columbia business school in NYC after high school."

"Ivy League? That's impressive, Hayes."

"It was great. I loved it there. Then I landed a job with my firm located right in the city after college, and I've been there since. Though, what I'm doing now, traveling around and buying companies, is a new branch of our firm which I actually helped start. One of my father's friends owned a very successful souvenir shop back home. The friend landed on some hard times with his health and couldn't maintain the shop, so I designed a plan to buy it so he'd walk away with a nice check that would help him cover his medical expenses and bills for a long time. I convinced my firm that these locally-owned places in small towns are good investments. They trusted me, and the rest is history."

"Oh, wow," I say.

"Yeah, I know I can come off as the bad guy...lurking around communities and buying out businesses that have been in families for generations, but that isn't why I do it. My intention is to buy places that have become a burden, stores where the owners want to sell for varying personal reasons. My ultimate goal is to help."

I think about his words, and I know they're true. Hayes is a good person. "I see that. And for the record, I never saw you as a bad guy."

"Well, I'm glad. You're the last person I'd want to see me that way." His voice deepens, causing the goose bumps on my arms to resurface.

My head feels fuzzy and dueling emotions leave me feeling confused. I swallow the lump in my throat. "We should get back. The nurse's shift is almost over."

I turn on my heel to face the other direction and speed walk home.

Chapter Fourteen

"Have a great day, Susie," I tell my local caramel supplier as she leaves. Opening the bag of fresh caramels, I pour them into the glass container holding the same candy.

"Ooh, new caramels," Hayes says from behind me.

"Yeah, you just missed Susie, my supplier. Try one." I hand him a wrapped candy.

He shakes his head. "Not really a fan. Too hard. Gets stuck in my teeth." He opens his mouth in an awkward smile and points toward his pearly whites.

I laugh. "That's why I want you to try these. They aren't hard at all, just creamy and amazing."

"Fine." He takes the candy from my outstretched hand, unwraps it, and pops it into his mouth. After a couple of chews, his eyes go wide, and he nods. "Mm-hmm."

"Right? So good." I close the caramel container and throw the bag out. "I was thinking today we could..."

Hayes lifts his hand, halting my thoughts. "Don't mean to interrupt, but I actually just came in to tell you I'll be leaving for a couple of days."

I tilt my head to the side.

"Yeah, sorry it's last minute. I have to fly down to Key West. One of the companies I've been working with is ready to sell, and they want to do it quickly. I guess the husband, who is the one I've been communicating with, passed away, and after his death, the wife found out he had been cheating on her for thirty years. She wants to sell his store and take a cruise around the world with her male friend from the church choir. It's a whole long thing." He waves his hand.

"Wow. I guess so," I say with a laugh. "Your job is like having a front-row seat to a dramatic soap opera."

"Sometimes it is." He nods. "I hope to be back by tomorrow night or the following morning."

"Okay, I can take you to the airport."

"No, it's a couple of hours each way. I won't take up that much of your time. I'll just call a taxi or Uber. Does this town have Uber?"

I raise a brow. "Do you know how much the fare for that trip would be? Here." I grab my car keys from the counter and toss them to Hayes. "Take my car."

"No. You might need it."

"Well, if I do, I can think of about a hundred people

who would loan me theirs, no questions asked. Take my car so you'll have a ride back, too."

"Okay, if you're sure?"

"I am."

"Thank you, Evie. Try to hold down the fort while I'm gone." He shoots me an adorable smile as he turns to leave.

"I'll try."

Hayes is leaving for two days, and I already know I'm going to miss him. I can't miss someone I don't have. His presence here is part of his job, and I understand this. Yet when we're together, it feels like more. There's a friendship there, a familiarity, a connection. Am I imagining something deeper because I crave someone to be closer with?

Regardless, I need to stop. Hayes is going to be gone before I know it and not just for two days. For good. Nothing will change that, so whatever I'm starting to feel needs to end now. I'm dealing with enough heartache in my life. I don't need anymore.

The day flies by with a flurry of new customers. Cherry picking hasn't officially started, but the town is full of visitors.

"Thank you so much. Enjoy!" I hand a gift-wrapped package of goodies over the counter to a young couple on their honeymoon.

After they've left the shop, the phone rings. It's my friend Cal from the bakery.

"Evie!"

"Hey, Cal. What's up?"

"I need you to swing by the bakery as soon as you can. Please."

"Um, okay. Sure," I say.

I hang up the phone and call up to the nurse to let her know I'm heading out for a minute. Before leaving the shop, I hang the sign on the front door that says, "Out on a top secret mission. Be back in a few. Make sure to claim your free licorice stick for your wait when I get back."

The sign has a guy in a spacesuit straddling a spaceship made of candy. The flames coming out of the back of the spaceship are licorice sticks. The ship is flying toward a moon made from a gumball. It was a gift to Pops from Sweetie for Christmas when I was ten. It was meant to be a gag gift, but he loved it and used it every time he had to step out, and we've continued to use it.

It's another thing Hayes doesn't understand. He says that our store has nothing to do with space, and the sign is random. He also thinks it's weird that a business will simply lock its doors and leave in the middle of the day to run errands. All valid points but nothing I would change. Adventures often come from the randomness life sends our way.

I walk down Main Street and peek into several stores

on my way to say hi to friends before reaching the bakery.

The bakery is owned by my friend Cal Bennett's parents. Cal has grown up here and is in charge of all of the decorating now. He's so talented and could make a cake into pretty much anything.

The smell of sweet bread and frosting hits me as I step through the front door.

"Evie." Cal waves from behind the glass display case.

"Hey, what's up?" I ask.

"I'm so sorry. Ma sprained her ankle this morning, and Dad had to drive her to the city to get X-rays and all of that. I know you paid for delivery, but it's just been me here today, and it's been so busy. Have you been crazy today, too? Aren't there an abnormal amount of people here? I can't keep up. Then again, that could just be because I'm a one-man operation here."

I hold up my hand, urging Cal to take a breath. "I'm sorry. I'm confused. What are you talking about?"

"Your cupcakes. I wasn't able to deliver them."

I squint my eyes. "I didn't order any cupcakes."

He grabs a ticket from a drawer. "Ma took the order, but it clearly says your name and twenty cupcakes, two of every kind we carry." He disappears into the back room and returns with a large cardboard box. Walking around the counter, he hands it to me. "Once again, I'm sorry I couldn't deliver them. I just haven't been able to leave all day, and I didn't want to make you wait any longer. Do you want me to throw in a loaf of bread or some muffins to make up for the delivery charge?"

"No." I shake my head, confused.

"I'm sorry. I'll refund you."

"No." I pull my stare from the box. "It's not a big deal, Cal. Really." I look at the line that's already formed behind me. "I should go and let you get back to it. Thank you so much for these."

He nods and shoots me a quick smile, then he's moved on to assist the person behind me. I walk back home. Once in the shop, I place the box of cupcakes on the counter and open it. There are twenty big and delicious-looking cupcakes inside. There's also a note.

I quickly open it up.

Evie,

I wasn't sure what your favorite flavor was. So, I got you a sampling.

I'll miss you while I'm away.

Eat a cupcake for me.

-H

I stare at the words on the card over and over again. The longer I stare, the more confused I become. The gesture is sweet, and the note is innocent, I think. It's the line, *I'll miss you while I'm away*, that has me confused. Do business partners miss each other? Friends can miss each other. And Hayes has become a good friend. That's all it is. A note and a kind gesture from a friend.

Yeah, that's all it is.

I take a big bite of a chocolate cherry cupcake and groan as the goodness hits my mouth.

Chapter Fifteen

I've always loved walking down Main Street. The old brick buildings with their decorated seasonal storefront window displays match the festive trees that line the street. The branches have lost all of their pink and white petals of spring and now carry the bright green leaves of summer.

Everyone who visits Cherry Blossom Grove says people write stories about this kind of town, and Hallmark features this kind of town in their Christmas specials. For most, this place is surreal, a dream, an escape, but for me, it's reality. I make an effort to remind myself that living here is a gift, and I never want to take it for granted. And I don't feel I do. Even though it's all I've ever known, I know it's special.

I wave at the townsfolk I pass, most of whom I've known all of my life. I also greet the new faces, the visitors, and some who are seeing this place for the first time.

Everyone seems happy. Sunshine and warmth fill my lungs, and I can't help but smile. Summers are our shortest season this far north, and perhaps that's why it's my favorite.

I turn toward the decorative town square, past the fountain, and to the doors of Amigos. "Evie." My name is called, and I twist to face its source.

"Hazel, hi."

She walks up next to me and pulls me into a hug. "How are you?"

"Great. You?"

"Same." We release each other from the embrace and walk through the front doors of the restaurant.

"I've barely eaten anything all day, so I could pig out tonight. I'm starving," Hazel exclaims.

"Me too," I say, waving toward some of our friends sitting at our usual table toward the back of the restaurant.

Matty and Abby are already here and are seated across from Audrey and Callan.

"Cal?" I whisper to Hazel as we approach the table.

"Yeah, I invited him. I don't know. I'm feeling it out. Be cool," she says under her breath, and I laugh.

Hazel and Cal have had an on-again, off-again thing going for years. I wouldn't even classify it as a relationship, more like a flirtation.

Hazel and I greet the group with a round of hugs, and I let her take the seat at the end of the table beside

Cal and Matty. I sit at the other end between Abby and Audrey.

Señora Fernandez, Matty's mother, stops by the table and chats with us for a couple of minutes before taking our orders.

Abby and Matty update us on all of the preparations at the cherry orchard. Hazel tells us what she's been up to at the winery. Cal gives us the latest happenings at the bakery. Audrey talks about plans to put in a heated pool at the end of the season at the bed and breakfast.

"It's a shame they couldn't fit us in before the season this year, but it will be nice for our autumn guests," Audrey says.

Autumn is actually fairly busy as the town gets many tourists coming through on tours when the leaves start changing colors.

Señora Fernandez brings us our drinks.

After she's left, Audrey turns to me. "How's the shop? You only have a couple of weeks left, right?"

I take a long swig of my water. "Yep, two weeks and then I'm done."

"How are you feeling about that?" Abby asks.

I ponder her question for a moment. "Good. I think."

"That's good. You deserve to do whatever makes you happy." Abby smiles.

Aubrey taps my arm. "Yeah, the guests at the B&B rave about your photos. Seriously, they can't stop talking about how happy they are with them."

"Really?" My chest fills with pride.

"Absolutely." Aubrey nods. "You really scored with Hayes and his people skills. I swear all he talks about is you." She chuckles. "His admiration for you is contagious. He has this way of chatting up your photography skills over a meal without sounding salesy and the guests end up asking him if he can get them a session with you."

"Aw." Hazel sighs, her sentiment mirroring my own.

Aubrey raises her brows and catches me in her stare. "Speaking of Hayes. He's gorgeous and successful, and you work side by side with him every day."

"And?" I question.

"Don't be coy, Evie. You know what I'm getting at. What's going on with you two?" Aubrey questions.

I shrug. "Nothing. We're friends and business associates. It's all very professional."

She shakes her head. "I don't buy that for a minute. No one talks about someone the way he talks about you and not have feelings."

"It doesn't matter," I say. "He's leaving in two weeks."

Abby leans in closer, her eyes wide. "So there *are* feelings?"

"I don't know. He's wonderful to be around. We have a lot of fun working together. He's been so helpful to Sweetie and me in so many ways, but I don't allow myself to really think about what that all means because he's leaving. So, it doesn't matter. I'm never moving away from here, and his job requires him to travel all over. It would be pointless to even imagine there could be more.

Okay? Are you all satisfied?" One corner of my mouth tilts up.

My female friends sigh. "Fine." Abby pouts. "I guess you're right. There's really no point."

"Exactly," I say.

"Well, it was fun to think about," Aubrey says. "I mean, it's been so long since you've provided us with any fun gossip."

I laugh. "I'm sorry my life is so a boring. Please enlighten us with some of your wild adventures."

"Well." Quirking a brow and puckering her lips, Aubrey looks around the table, catching everyone's attention. She's a master at building suspense. "There was this guy, Brock, that stayed with us last week. He was a wine vendor, hotter than hot. Right?"

Señora Fernandez returns with a tray full of food.

"Oh, thank you, Mamá, for saving us from what I'm sure would've been a very graphic and uncomfortable story to listen to." He looks at Aubrey with a mock grimace.

"Hey! At least I have some juicy tales to tell. The rest of you are a tad boring, if I'm being honest," she protests.

"I like boring," Cal says to Aubrey before thanking Señora Fernandez.

Abby taps Aubrey's hand. "Maybe your adventure with the hottie wine vendor is more suitable for a night out with just the girls."

Hazel agrees. "Yeah, I definitely want to hear all

about it. I met Brock when he came by the vineyard. We'll have to get the details of that story when we do a girls' night."

We eat our meals and chat about topics not related to Aubrey's love life. It's wonderful to see my friends. We're all such hard workers and always so busy. I truly cherish the times we can get together. I've known everyone at this table since kindergarten, and I know we'll be lifelong friends.

I eat until my stomach is full and laugh until my sides ache. In this space, my worries dissipate, and I simply feel happy. Friendships are good for the soul.

Chapter Sixteen

I scroll through the pictures I took of a sweet couple and their "baby," which was a very large and fluffy Old English sheepdog named Max. The photos turned out great, and Max is stealing the show in every picture. This will be my family photo one day, except there will be no man, and the dog will be a grouchy orange cat.

That's okay. At least I'll have Pumpkin whether he likes it or not. So I won't be alone.

"Those are really good." Hayes peers over my shoulder.

"Thanks. I'm kind of obsessed with Max."

"Max?"

"The dog."

"Gotcha. Well, he is adorable."

"Tell me, Hayes. Are you a dog person or a cat person?" I ask.

"That's a hard one. I like both. I grew up with both. If I had to choose, I would say that I enjoy the company of dogs a little more than cats, but it's close. What about you?"

"I don't know. We've never had pets, probably since we've always lived in an apartment. Pumpkin showed up as a homely little kitten shortly after Pops died. Sweetie couldn't turn him away. I think it had something to do with his bright orange hair, which is almost identical to my grandfather's hair. I love Pumpkin, but I don't know anything else. Growing up, I dreamed of having dogs and ponies, and all matter of furry creatures. I even tried befriending a raccoon that frequented the dumpster out back for one summer."

Hayes smiles. "Well, I can tell you that not all cats are like Pumpkin. Cats are all so different, and they're born with a distinct personality. Sometimes you luck out and get a super sweet one, and sometimes you can get a big jerk. Whereas dogs are always sweet and live for their owners. My sister and I got to pick out kittens from the local shelter for our eighth birthday. I got a tabby striped little guy and named him Obi Wan. My sister got this long-haired black cat and named him Whiskers, very original. Obi was the nicest cat in the universe, whereas Whiskers was Satan incarnate. You just never know. I'd get cats all day long if they were all like Obi."

"Whiskers was that bad?" I laugh.

"Maybe I'm exaggerating a little. Hattie would tell

you that I am, but that cat was only nice to her. He hated the rest of the family."

"I want a dog someday," I say.

"You can have a dog and live in an apartment. People do it all of the time. You just have to walk it regularly."

"Yeah, I can do that. Now that I won't be in the shop all day, I'll have more time."

"Right," he agrees.

He steps beside me and opens up his laptop. "Audrey tells me that you went out while I was in Florida, had a date night. That's good."

"I wouldn't call it a date." I scoff. "It was a dinner with friends. I haven't had a real date since I was in high school."

"That's right! Senior prom, if I remember correctly? I honestly still can't believe that."

"It's true. I mean, my pops died when I was nineteen, and I've been busy helping Sweetie since then. Plus, there just isn't anyone in my life I want to date. I've known every guy my age here since I was five. If someone here was meant for me, I'd already know it."

"Seven years. You haven't been on a real date in seven years?" Hayes questions with utter disbelief lining his voice.

"Stop saying it like it's weird," I protest.

Hayes lifts a brow. "It's a little odd."

"Well, I went to Amigos on that business dinner with you," I offer.

"That was a business dinner. Not a real date."

"Anyway." I shrug. "I'm thinking about taking the couple celebrating their fiftieth anniversary to the vineyard for some shots."

"Uh, no." Hayes shakes his head. "You are not changing the subject like that. We're not done with this no date in seven years conversation."

"Ugh," I groan. "I'm sorry I said anything. Can we just table it?"

"I have a better idea." The corners of Hayes's lips tilt up. "How about I take you on a date? A real date so you can no longer say you haven't been on a date in seven years."

"You're asking me on a date?"

"Yeah."

"I don't know, Hayes." I hesitate. "It's asking for issues. We should keep our relationship professional. You're here to buy my business. I don't want to make things awkward."

"It won't be awkward," Hayes reassures me. "It'll just be a friendly date between co-workers."

"Co-workers?" I chuckle.

"Well, we are at the moment. Wouldn't you say?"

I think about it. "Yeah, I suppose we are. What will we do on this little co-worker outing?"

"I don't know...yet, and if I did, I wouldn't say. It's a surprise. That's part of the fun in having a date, right?"

The bell above the shop door jingles, pulling us away

from our date conversation. Mrs. Snively enters in a flurry.

"Evie," she calls.

"Good morning, Mrs. Snively," I greet her.

Her eyes dart around the shop. "I need..." She paces down the first aisle of candy.

I step around the corner at the other end of the aisle and come face-to-face with her. "Mrs. Snively, why don't you tell me what you're looking for, and I can help you find it."

She takes a big breath. "Well, we have the silent auction tomorrow at church to raise money for the new children's wing at the library. Annabelle Evans signed up to donate a few baskets, but apparently, she forgot all about it because when I asked her about it this morning, she acted like she had no idea what I was talking about! So, now we're short on auction items. I was hoping you had some themed baskets in here I could get to donate."

"I can put together a few themed baskets and drop them off at the church this afternoon," I suggest.

"Oh, really? That would be lovely, dear. It's just I'm very busy organizing the event for tomorrow, and when people sign up for things but don't come through, it makes it very stressful for me."

I place my hands on the sides of her arms in a distant embrace. "Don't even worry one more second. I'll take care of it."

She fans her face and blows out a breath. "Oh, thank you, Evie. You're a godsend."

"I don't know what I'm going to do when you sell this place." She presses her forefingers against her cheeks and sighs.

"Hayes here will make sure the new owners are well versed in customer satisfaction," I reassure her.

"I hope you do." She directs her statement toward Hayes.

"Why don't you head back over to the church, and I'll take care of everything here. I know you're busy," I say.

"Oh, I am. Very busy. Thank you, dear." She turns on her heels and speed walks toward the door. Before she exits, she looks back. "If you could have them to me by three o'clock, it would be appreciated."

"I will have them to you by two," I respond.

"Even better." she nods.

"See you soon." I wave as she exits the shop.

I walk back over to Hayes.

"She's a delight," he deadpans.

"She means well." I chuckle. "Admittedly, she's a little high strung."

"A little?"

"Not everyone handles stress well." I press my lips together. "Would you like me to show you where I keep everything for the gift baskets?"

"Sure," Hayes quips, his tone overly excited.

"Sometimes people request baskets for birthdays or special events, like the auction. So, I keep an eye out for themed items that are on sale throughout the year that would look cute with candy, and I store them back here." I lead Hayes to the storage closet. "I love making the baskets. They always turn out so cute."

I point at the cherry section of the shelving unit and grab a handmade basket with woven cherries around the perimeter. "Obviously, the cherry theme is very popular here." I grab a cherry mug and other themed goodies.

"Obviously." Hayes chuckles.

"What other theme shall we do? There's Disney, Snoopy, bumblebees, school." I start listing the possible basket themes.

"How about date night?"

"Oh, that could be a fun one. Let me see if I have anything that could go with it." I pull down a basket of random things from the shelf.

"I'm talking about our date night," Hayes says.

"Fine." I give in because I know he's not going to drop it. "Just a friendly co-worker date."

I feel the need to clarify because I don't want any mixed messages. There's no point in pretending this date is anything other than what it is...Hayes being nice. He's the type of guy who would take a girl out on a special date because she hasn't been out on one in seven years. As endearing as that is, I can't overthink it because, in two weeks, he'll be gone.

"Awesome." Hayes claps his hands together, startling me. "Well, I have to run. I'll pick you up tonight at seven."

He turns and exits the storage closet.

"Uh, okay," I say, confused.

"Have fun with Mrs. Snively this afternoon," he calls out before leaving the shop.

"Bye," I say under my breath because Hayes is already gone.

I'm left standing here wondering if I just made a mistake.

No, it will be fine.

Totally fine.

Chapter Seventeen

Skinny jeans, a black tank top, and a pair of flip-flops taunt me. I twist to the side and stare at my reflection in the full-length mirror on the back of my bedroom door. Too much? Not enough? I don't know. I want my outfit to scream, *I care about my appearance and am thankful for your kind gesture but in no way am I trying to impress you because we are just co-workers, and soon you'll be gone.*

I don't want to look like a slob, but I also don't want to appear too invested.

I throw my hands up in the air. "It's fine, Evie. Jeez."

Turning to Pumpkin, who lays on my bed, I say, "It's a good choice, right? Simple, classy, not overstated?"

In response, he lifts his leg and starts to clean himself.

"Gee, thanks." I roll my eyes. "It's good," I decide.

My long red hair hangs down my back in natural

waves. I always wear it in a ponytail, so I figured the least I could do for this date was to wear it down. It just seems more mature, and I am definitely that. Nothing screams maturity like a platonic date with a business partner.

I put on some lip gloss and grab my handbag. "Come out and keep Sweetie company," I tell Pumpkin.

Sweetie sits in her rocking recliner watching *Golden Girls*. Christine, her nurse, has graciously agreed to stay late tonight in exchange for taking Monday off.

"I can't thank you enough," I say to Christine.

"Oh, this works out perfect for me. I had completely forgotten about my granddaughter's dental appointment on Monday. I promised my daughter-in-law that I could take her. We're going to have a granny, granddaughter day."

"That does sound like fun," I say. "Well, you know the deal. If you need anything, call. Dinner is in the crockpot when you two get hungry. Help yourself to anything in the refrigerator."

"Will do." Christine shoots me a grin. "You just enjoy yourself."

"Thank you," I say as a soft knock sounds on the door. I hurry over to Sweetie and give her a kiss on the cheek. "Bye." I wave to them both as I make my way toward the door.

When I open it, Hayes is standing there with a grand bouquet of Gerbera daisies in bright shades of orange, yellow, pink, and red. I pull in a breath as he hands the bouquet over. Gerbera daisies are my favorite flowers.

They're just so...*happy*. I can't help but feel joy when I look at them.

"Thank you! These are my favorite." I take the bouquet from him.

"I know." He smiles.

Peering under the sink, I find our vase and pull it out. "How do you know that?"

"You mentioned it once," he states.

I fill the vase with water and set the flowers inside. They really are beautiful. "Wow, I don't even remember that conversation."

"It wasn't as much of a conversation as a brief comment attached to another conversation, but you'll find that I remember everything about you, Evie Emberton." he proclaims.

His declaration stirs up a foreign emotion within me. "Well, they are lovely. Thank you."

He stands to the side of the door, and I grab my purse off the counter and take a step past him. "What's on the agenda tonight?"

He closes the door and follows me down the stairs. "All in good time."

"You're not going to tell me?" I chuckle.

"What would be the fun in that?"

I follow Hayes out to a red Mustang convertible, and he opens the passenger door for me. "Is this Ben Stanford's car?" Only one person in town owns a car like this.

"It is. I borrowed it."

"How do you know Ben?"

I put my seat belt on as Hayes walks around the front of the car and slides into the driver's seat.

"You're not the only one with friends in this town, Ms. Evie." He smirks playfully, and I can't help but laugh.

I hold my hair in my hands as he pulls onto the road. The warm summer air tingles against my skin as he accelerates.

He peers over at me. "All right. Let's talk about goals for the night?"

"Goals?"

"Yes, you are the hardest worker I know. You're always busting your butt for everyone around you. Tonight the goal is just to relax and have fun. No stress. No worries. Got it?"

"I think I can handle that," I say.

Hayes turns onto the long country road leading out of town. Acres of cornfields without a car in sight. In a couple of months, the short cornstalks will be taller than Hayes.

"Okay, for your first challenge. I need you to sit up on your knees," he says.

"What?" I whip my head toward him.

"Just do it." He laughs. "Sit up on your knees, on the seat. Please."

"Fine." I do as instructed, my sigh getting lost in the wind.

When I sit raised higher in my seat, the wind hits against my face. I wrap my hair tightly around my hand.

"Now," Hayes yells out to me, "close your eyes. Extend your hands out to the side and just feel. Don't open your eyes until I say so. Okay?"

"Okay!" I shout nervously over the wind.

I steady myself against the back of the seat. Still on my knees, I close my eyes and release my arms to the sides. My hair whips around behind my head, and the air rushing past me pushes me back. We hit a bump, and I grab onto the door.

"You won't fall. I promise," Hayes reassures me.

I release the door and push down all feelings of doubt. I ignore the voice in my head that tells me I look silly because, at this moment, I don't want to hear it. I want to be free. Sitting up taller, I raise up on my knees, throw my hands to the sides, and let my head fall back as the wind hits my face. The car's engine revs as Hayes goes faster. The air tickles my skin as my hair whips around frantically. I bounce on my knees with the rolling waves of the pavement beneath us. I can't hear anything but the rush screaming in my ears. I feel like I'm skipping across the clouds. My smile grows, and I start to laugh.

The car goes faster, and I feel it speeding up a hill, and then as it dips hard on the descent, my knees lift off the seat, and I scream. I fall to the leather seats and grab onto the dashboard, laughing like a little girl.

I open my eyes to see Hayes smiling. "So fun, right?" he asks.

"So fun."

He turns on the radio, and we just drive. I hang my arm out to the side and wave it up and down in the air. I don't think of anything but this moment, driving with the wind in my hair and music around me. It's so simple yet so enjoyable.

Hayes has driven in a big circle and eventually slows down in front of Hazel's vineyard.

"We're visiting Hazel?" I ask.

"Not exactly," he says, turning into her drive. He passes her house and continues down the path beside the orchard. At the end of the rows of grapes sits a sky blue vintage truck.

Hayes parks in front of the truck, and we get out. My hair is a windblown, ratted mess. I take the hairband from my wrist and pull it into a messy bun.

The bed of the old truck is covered in blankets, and pillows propped against the back. There's a cooler and a basket of snacks. Facing the bed of the truck is a projector screen. The entire setup is straight from a magazine. I'm completely speechless as I circle the truck and take in all of the small details.

"This is incredible, Hayes." The astonishment in my voice is clear as I shake my head. "I don't even know what to say. This is so cool, and the truck is adorable."

"I borrowed the truck from farmer John. It's a 1950 Chevy. I thought it fit the theme."

"How do you know farmer John?"

I'm baffled at how he pulled off such a unique date with only an afternoon to plan, especially when he's only been in our town for a couple of weeks. John lives outside of town. He's a sweet man of at least eighty years old. He's always working on his land, so I barely see him. I'm trying to figure out how Hayes knows him.

"I talk to him every morning when he drops off the produce for the B&B. He's great," Hayes says.

"He is." I nod toward the projector. "So, movie night?"

"You guessed it."

"I can't believe you can get power out here," I say.

Hayes toes an orange cord on the ground. "A crazy long extension cord will do wonders."

A vehicle approaches, and I recognize it as Matty's car.

Matty parks and pulls two bags out of the car. "Hey, guys!" he says, walking toward us.

We greet him, and Hayes takes the bags from him and hands over some cash. "Thank you, Matt. Appreciate it, man."

"Anytime," Matty says to Hayes. "Have a great night." He waves to us both before hopping back in his car and backing out.

"Is that what I think it is?" I grin.

"It's your favorite, right?" Hayes smiles. "I got veggie fajitas with all the fixings, rice and beans, and of course, chips and salsa."

I clap my hands together. "That sounds amazing."

I climb up into the back of the truck, and Hayes follows. He sets out a fajita picnic before us, and I start dishing up. Opening the cooler, he pulls out a bottle of wine.

"Sangria? I figured a date in Hazel's family's orchard wouldn't be complete without some of their sangria."

"Yes, that sounds great."

He pours two glasses and hands me one. Dinner is delicious, and the conversation is pleasant. Everything with Hayes is always easy. He could talk with anyone like he's known them for years. He just has this way with people, evident by all the favors his new friends helped him with for tonight's date.

"Did your high school have some sort of a most likable category for your senior yearbook?" I ask him.

He finishes swallowing a big bite of fajita. "Yeah, it was called, *everyone's friend*."

"You were voted everyone's friend, weren't you?"

He puckers his lips, holding in a smile. "Yeah," he admits finally. "How did you know?"

I shrug. "I just knew it. I thought you told me once that you were serious as a child?"

"I was. Serious but friendly. I had a lot of friends, but I still don't think I had as many as you do. What were you voted as your senior year?" he asks.

"Um...I don't know," I mumble.

"You were voted most likable, too. Weren't you?" Hayes quirks a brow.

"Yeah." I sigh.

"Of course you were. You're the sweetest person I know. Why do you say it like it's a bad thing?"

Picking up a napkin, I wipe my mouth, then lean back against the pillows with my glass of wine. I've eaten all of the Mexican food my body can hold. "It's not a bad thing. Just, for my school, I felt like it was a blah category. Like, I'm nice. Woo-hoo. Most people here are nice."

"Yeah, but you were voted the nicest. That's definitely not blah. The other categories are meaningless really—most likely to succeed, hottest, best couple, class clown, best at sports—those are all perceptions or shallow. Looks fade or change over time, and true beauty begins on the inside anyway. What is success? None of those couples are still together. What makes a football player more talented than a volleyball player? How do people even decide who is best at sports? Right? Honestly, kindness is the most important thing in the world. As adults, no one cares if we were good at track in high school. But our hearts and our words can make someone's day."

"Yeah, that's true." I take a sip of my wine. "Were you voted anything else?" I ask Hayes.

"Most likely to succeed." Hayes chuckles.

"Such a golden boy." I grin. "Nicest and most likely to succeed. I'm not surprised. What do you think success is?"

"I don't personally equate success with money. I think a successful life is a happy life. Doing something you love and surrounding yourself with people you love. That's the dream. Isn't it?"

I nod. "That's a great dream."

"Are you ready for a movie?" he asks.

"Yeah, what are we watching?"

"Well, I brought choices. I have *Pretty in Pink, Sweet Home Alabama*, and *Thirteen Going on Thirty*."

"Nice." I approve. "Some classics."

"Also, I brought one of my favorites, and I don't know if you've seen it, but I think you'll love it." He holds up the disc. "*The Greatest Showman*."

"Oh, I've heard great things about that one, but I've never watched it. I've always wanted to, though."

He hops off the truck with *The Greatest Showman* in hand. "All right, well then, I think this is the winner because you will love this movie." Hayes sets up the film and gets back in the bed of the truck. He offers me some movie snacks.

"Maybe in a bit. I'm still so full from dinner," I say.

We lean back against the pillows and get lost in my new favorite movie because Hayes was right. I absolutely loved it.

Chapter Eighteen

When Hayes enters the shop the next morning, I have the soundtrack of *The Greatest Showman* blaring through the speakers as I sweep the floor. When I got back from our date last night, the first thing I did was purchase and download the soundtrack. I'm already obsessed.

He just shakes his head with a smile.

"Why did I never watch that movie before? I'm literally obsessed. Do you want to watch it again tonight upstairs with Sweetie? She'll love the music."

"Sure," Hayes says.

"Is that crazy?" I laugh at myself.

"No, I watched it back-to-back the first time I saw it, too." Hayes makes me feel better with his statement.

Truthfully, I'm still on cloud nine from the friend date with Hayes last night. It's been so long since I went out and was not worried about anything back home or with the store. I forgot what that feeling was like. And it felt good. I needed it. Hayes knew it, too. I'm so grateful for him and his kindness. Despite getting very little sleep last night, I feel energized today.

I turn down the music so I don't have to yell over it. "I stayed up way too late googling everything about that movie. Have you seen the YouTube clips of Hugh Jackman singing 'From Now On,' and Keala Settle singing 'This is Me' during their read-through in New York City?"

"I have. Incredible."

I put the broom back into the closet. "So incredible. Like those clips gave me chills. I watched them both several times. Thank you again for such an amazing night. I didn't realize how much I needed it until today. Life has been so heavy as of late, and today, I feel so much better."

"I'm so glad, and you're absolutely welcome. I had a great time, too." He meets me around the counter. "What's on the agenda for today?"

"I don't know." I chuckle. "The weekend nurse is upstairs with Sweetie, so I'm free to show you anything you still need to know. It should be fairly busy today, given that it's a Saturday and the church is having the auction, which will bring people into town. Is there anything you want to learn about?"

Hayes thinks for a moment. "Yes. I'd like to see Mrs. Snively run that church auction. Let's get through the morning rush of people here at the shop, and then play hooky and go check out the auction."

"We can't close the shop down on a Saturday," I say.

"Sure we can. Let's put up your little moon man, top secret mission sign and head out. Come on, it will be fun," Hayes urges.

"Mrs. Snively is entertaining."

"I figured she was. Plus, I want to see what the good people of Cherry Blossom Grove put up for auction. I bet there are some real finds." He winks.

"Fine," I relent. "But not until at least two. We'll still catch plenty of the auction."

"I can agree to two o'clock," Hayes says before stepping around the counter to greet a couple of customers that just came in. They're tourists as I've never seen them before. I watch Hayes speak to them effortlessly. He makes some joke about Tootsie Rolls, and they laugh.

I sure am going to miss his energy around here when he leaves.

* * *

"Who would want this?" Hayes says under his breath.

He's staring at a very colorful plastic parrot clock that croaks out a high pitched, "Good day, mate!" every hour. It's the oddest cuckoo clock I've ever seen.

"A Jimmy Buffett fan?" I suggest.

"I'm going to bid a penny." He reaches for a bidding slip.

"No." I laugh, tapping his hand. "Don't. What if you're the only bid and Mrs. Snively has to come after you to collect the penny? How embarrassing."

"True. She probably wouldn't be very happy with a one-cent bid."

"Probably not."

He reaches toward the next item on the table. It's a snowman made of someone's white athletic tube sock. "What about this?" He grins, holding the snowman up. The sock bends in half, and the head of the snowman flops down toward its feet.

"I'm pretty sure I made one of those in first grade." I tilt my head to the side to stare at the sad snowman.

"Mr. Watson! We look with our eyes, not our hands," Mrs. Snively chastises as she takes the sock snowman from Hayes's grasp and places it down on the table.

"I'm sorry, Mrs. Snively. I just wanted to get a better look. I'm very interested in bidding on it." Hayes attempts to throw some charm her way.

"That is all fine and good, but look with your eyes from now on, please," she snaps before her attention is torn away from us, and she storms across the room to correct some other unsuspecting soul.

As soon as she's gone, we start to laugh. "I feel like a kid in trouble." Hayes shakes his head.

"Well, that's because you're not looking with your eyes!" I whisper-shout, trying to keep a straight face.

He holds up his hands in surrender. "Lesson

learned, and you're right. I don't want her coming after me to collect a penny bid."

"Right?"

We continue to stroll down the tables of auction items.

"This looks like your size." Hayes points at a T-shirt that says, *She's my cherry pie,* but the cherry is a picture of a cherry, and the pie is the symbol for pi in mathematics. "It incorporates your love for cherries and math. I'm sure you care a great deal about the ratio of the distance around the circle to the circle's diameter."

"Actually, this might come as a surprise to you, but I do not." I chuckle.

"Do you remember what pi is?" Hayes asks.

"I know it's 3.14 and then a whole string of numbers. We had this competition in sixth grade to see who could remember the most numbers in pi. Needless to say, I didn't come close to winning."

"Yeah, we had the same competition."

I turn toward Hayes. "You won. Didn't you?"

Hayes laughs. "Yeah."

"How many numbers did you memorize?"

"It was like thirty."

"That's impressive. That right there is what made you a shoo-in for 'most likely to succeed' in high school."

"That must be it." He grins. "But, seriously, is there anything here worth bidding on?"

I scan the room, "Yeah, usually there are a few cool things. The local travel agent always donates a weekend trip, Abby usually donates a bunch of cherry desserts, Hazel always provides a large basket of wine, and some of the other small businesses donate gift cards."

"So no trips to Paris or gentleman's daysailer yacht?" Hayes asks.

Just when I think he couldn't get cooler, he does when he references one of my favorite episodes of *Friends*. "This isn't a Ralph Lauren auction."

"Why did I not know that you're a *Friends* fan?"

"I don't know because I've seen every episode at least ten times. It's surprising that Gerbera daisies came up but not *Friends*." I pick up a mug to get a better look and see that it is indeed just a ceramic tree stump with a handle. "Tree stump mug?" I ask Hayes.

"Look with your eyes, Miss Emberton!" Mrs. Snively chastises from across the church hall.

"Sorry!" I call out and quickly place the mug down. "Let's go see the petting zoo."

"The church auction has a petting zoo?" Hayes questions.

"Of course. Don't they all?" The corner of my mouth tilts up. "One of the local farmers, Mr. Bailey, brings animals every year. He has this pet llama named Willoughby, and he's like the cutest thing ever. Mr. Bailey trims his fur to look like he has this fluffy lion's mane around his head. It's adorable."

"Lead the way." Hayes extends his arm.

We walk through the church hall toward the door that leads to the back parking lot. We step outside. The makeshift fencing that Mr. Bailey set up is only a few feet in front of us, and Willoughby is staring right at us. His fluffy mane is as cute as ever.

"You weren't understating his adorableness. That is the coolest llama-lion I've ever seen." Hayes steps toward Willoughby.

"Be careful, he..." I haven't finished my warning before Willoughby spits a big glob of wetness right at Hayes's face. "Spits." I throw my head back and laugh as Hayes quickly scoots away from the llama, wiping his face.

"What the heck?" Hayes scoffs, wiping his face.

"Sorry. I tried to warn you. He does that."

"Why would a spitting llama be part of a petting zoo? Isn't spitting a defense mechanism to warn people away? I don't think he likes people." Hayes chuckles.

"No, he loves people. He also just loves to spit. It's part of his charm. We're all used to it. See that cloth hanging from Mr. Bailey's pocket?" I point toward the farmer. "It's to wipe off Willoughby's spit."

Hayes presses his hand to his forehead and moves his face from side to side. "This town never ceases to amaze me." He grins. "There's seriously no place like it. Every day, I learn a new astonishing fact about it. Today, I've discovered that you all auction off the weirdest stuff I've ever seen and enjoy being spit at."

"In fairness, I wouldn't say we enjoy the spit. We just know to move." I approach Willoughby and pet his nose. He nuzzles into my hand, enjoying the affection before he raises his head up and prepares to spit. I jump to the side. His spit misses me and falls onto the pavement. "See. You just have to be quick."

"Agility. Yes, also a requirement at petting zoos." Hayes presses his lips in a line.

I look over and see the piglets on the other end of the pen. "Let's go get Sweetie. The petting zoo is her favorite part of the church auction. Pigs are her favorite animal."

"Sounds good," Hayes agrees.

"We'll let the nurse go home early, then spend some time with Sweetie and the animals, order a veggie pizza, and have a relaxed movie night. Deal?"

"I can't think of anything better," Hayes says with sincerity.

"Me either."

Chapter Nineteen

I stand under the showerhead, letting the water pelt my face. It's oddly refreshing. The warm water has carried the little stress still hovering around me down the drain and left me a pool of contentment. I'm simply happy. My stressors still exist, yet they don't consume me as they did just weeks ago. I can't deny that Hayes is to thank.

Work carries all of the responsibility it always has, yet I look forward to going downstairs every morning. Hayes and I have so much fun working in the shop. He's scored me so many photo sessions that I consider myself a legitimate photographer now. Sweetie isn't remarkably better, but we're getting by, and the nurse has been amazing.

Turning off the shower, I step out and get ready for my day. *The Greatest Showman's* soundtrack plays from the Bluetooth speakers, and I brush my hair and pull it into a ponytail. I'm one hundred percent obsessed with this soundtrack, and I don't even care. It, too, makes me happy.

"Today we shall do pink." I grab a pink ribbon and wrap it around my ponytail, tying it in a bow. Stepping out into the living room, I wrap my arms around Sweetie and kiss her cheek.

"Good morning. You're up early today," I say to her.

She doesn't respond, which is becoming her usual response as of late. Christine says that it's normal for Sweetie to talk less and less. I hate it, but I try not to think about it too much since there's nothing I can do.

"I'm going to make us some pancakes with bananas and chocolate like you used to make us on Sunday mornings. I always loved those mornings," I say to Sweetie. "Remember that time that Pops wanted to serve you breakfast in bed for your birthday and insisted on making the pancakes himself, but he added like ten times the amount of salt he was supposed to? I still don't know what he did. He said he mixed up tablespoons with teaspoons, but even then, they wouldn't have been that salty. It really didn't make sense. All I know is that I've never tried a more inedible pancake in my life. You tried so hard to eat it so you didn't hurt his feelings, but you just couldn't do it." I chuckle at the memory.

I try to talk to Sweetie about Pops as much as I can. He's her main anchor to reality. She never really responds, but I feel like it comforts her to hear stories about him anyway.

A knock sounds on the door as I'm plating Sweetie's pancakes. I open it to find Hayes.

"Good morning. Everyone's an early riser today, I see." I step to the side and invite him in. "Perfect timing, though, because I just made some of Sweetie's famous banana and chocolate pancakes."

"Well, I did eat at the B&B, but I guess I could squeeze a pancake down. They sound like something I don't want to miss."

"Oh, you don't. They're amazing." I carry Sweetie's plate to the table and set her up for breakfast.

"I also met one of CBG's most colorful people this morning," Hayes says when I get back into the kitchen.

"Oh, yeah? Who's that?" I plate up another pancake.

"Mrs. Snively, of course."

I look at Hayes. "Why did you meet up with Mrs. Snively?"

"Turns out, I won some bids at the auction." He holds up a bag.

"Really?" I set the plate down. "What did you win?"

He puts the bag on the counter. "Well, they're actually both for you. But don't get all bent out of shape because this first one only cost me a dollar. And I can tell you that showing up to give Mrs. Snively a dollar bill was just as awkward as if I had bid a penny." He shakes his head and pulls out the *She's my Cherry Pie* T-shirt.

I throw my head back in laughter. "You actually bid on that?"

"I told you that I'm a sixth-grade pi master. I had to

155

bid, but seeing that it won't fit me, it's yours." He hands the shirt to me.

"Thank you," I say. "I will wear it with pride."

"And I don't know why I bid on the next one. It just really reminded me of you." He pulls out a jewelry box, and I can't breathe. "I love the vines and the thorns. They emit this feeling of strength and power, and then the flowers are so delicate and beautiful. The whole box is this complex contradiction, so gorgeous and so tough at the same time. Like you." He hands me the box.

I stare at it, my heart beating rapidly in my chest. I don't know what to say.

Hayes squints his eyes. "Do you hate it?"

I shake my head. "I want to show you something," I say before turning away from Hayes and walking toward my room. Hayes follows me. "There was this local artist who created these jewelry boxes. They're quite the collector items now that he's gone, but even when he was alive, it was always difficult to get one as he had a very long waiting list."

I don't know if Hayes knows the history behind the box in my hands, and I don't say it aloud, but I know he spent a lot more than a dollar on it. These always go for a lot of money. I set the box he gave me down next to one by the same artist on my dresser. They're similar with vines, thorns, and flowers but also different as each box that the artist made was unique.

"You have one?" Hayes whispers, surprised.

"My pops got it for me for my sixteenth birthday,

and before he gave it to me, he said something very similar to what you just said to me in the kitchen."

In the time I've known Hayes, there have been these moments where I feel that Pops is speaking through him. Hayes will do or say something that Pops would've done or said—or has done or said in the past—and it throws me off because I don't know what to make of it. It feels like a sign, but a sign for what?

"I'm sorry. I'm confused. You don't seem to like it? Does it make you sad because it makes you think of your grandfather? I'm sorry if..."

I cut him off. "No, that's not it." I hesitate, thinking about how to best put my thoughts into the right words. "I love it. The box is beautiful, but it's too special of a gift for our situation."

"What situation is that?" he questions softly.

"You're leaving a week from tomorrow, right?" I ask.

"Yeah."

"Okay, then. We can't have a situation. You're leaving, and I'm staying."

"Evie." He lifts his arm and tucks a loose strand of hair that has fallen from my ponytail behind my ear.

I step back. "No, see...there's something, and I don't know what it is, but it can't be there. You're leaving," I repeat.

"I know." He lowers his head before returning his gaze to mine. "I'm leaving, but we're still friends. Right? Yes, we're doing business together, but given the nature of our arrangement, we've become friends, and that's okay. That's cool. There's nothing wrong with that situation."

"Hayes," I whisper.

"Evie, you have a million friends. I'm just one more. Sometimes friends get gifts for one another. That's what it is."

"That's all it is?"

"Of course," he says, but we both know that's not true.

It's something more, and I haven't let myself process what exactly, but the truth is, it doesn't matter.

He's leaving, and I'm staying.

"Are you sure about this? You could give it to Hattie or your mom?" I run my finger along the vine leading to a yellow daisy on the side of the jewelry box.

"I bought it for you. I want you to have it."

"Okay. Well, thank you. I love it."

"Can I still have a famous pancake?" He scrunches up his face.

"Absolutely. Come on."

We make our way back to the dining room where Sweetie sits, still slowly eating her breakfast. I warm the pancakes back up for Hayes, and we join her at the table.

"I'm glad that your month here falls over cherry-picking season. It'd be crazy if you bought a business in this town and never got the chance to actually go cherry picking. I was thinking about getting someone to watch the shop, and we can go tomorrow. Mondays are usually the least busy."

"Yeah, that sounds great," Hayes says through a mouthful of pancake. "These are incredible, by the way. Great recipe, Ms. Sweetie," he says to her.

"She's an amazing cook," I agree.

The weekend nurse arrives and joins us for breakfast.

"I also came over to tell you that I might not be able to join you at the shop today," Hayes says. "I have a few conference calls to make today. If I finish early, I can head back over, but realistically, I probably won't be able to."

"That's fine, but you do realize it's Sunday? Why are your meetings scheduled today?"

"Much like the candy shop business, my boss doesn't believe in days off when there is money to make. There are a lot of big sales coming up, and he wants to get everything figured out."

"Well, better today than tomorrow because you can't miss cherry picking," I say.

"I wouldn't dream of it."

His smile does something to me, but as usual, I choose to ignore it.

Chapter Twenty

It's a perfect early July day. Puffy clouds sprinkled throughout the clear blue sky provide just enough cover from the sun. In the mid-eighties, this is the extent of our heat during the summer months. The warmth against my skin feels nice, comforting.

I help Nana into the back seat, make sure she's buckled in and close the door while Hayes folds up her wheelchair and places it in the trunk.

"Thank you for coming with me," I say to him when he gets in the car. "I've never navigated the orchard with a wheelchair before, and Sweetie and I have never missed a cherry-picking season opening. I really appreciate it."

Hayes clicks his seat belt into place. "No thanks necessary. I'm excited to go to the big event."

We chose to go picking on a Monday. It will still be busy. Every day during cherry season is packed with people, but Mondays are a bit slower, especially when the cherries are still new at the start of the season.

"You sure Aidan can handle the shop?" Hayes asks.

I'm paying a local teen to man the store while we're gone. "Stop worrying. He'll be fine." I chuckle. "Mondays are pretty slow. In fact, when it's not cherry season, many businesses in Cherry Blossom Grove stay closed for the day."

"He's probably going to eat half the store. Did you see him eyeing the bin of gummy bears?"

I shake my head with a grin. "He does love the gummy candy."

"Evie," Hayes says, his voice laced with concern.

"Hayes, seriously. So the kid is going to eat a couple of pounds of gummy bears? Consider it part of his pay." I laugh. "You're a bit of a worrywart."

"I am not. I'm just not used to the lucid rules of business ownership in this town."

"Well, don't worry. Aidan is a great kid. He'll do a wonderful job, and he knows that I don't care if he eats some gummy bears. We have an understanding."

"If you say so. Everything will work out, right?" Hayes teases.

"Yes." I smile. "There's the spirit!"

We pull into the orchard and park the car. Hayes retrieves the wheelchair from the back, and I help Sweetie out of the back seat. She sits down in the wheelchair with a grumble.

"I really hate this, Evelyn. I'm fully capable of walking," she gripes, and it's music to my ears. She's barely said two words in several days, so I love hearing her voice. I've always thought that cherry picking was so special, and today just proves it. The beautiful scenery, fresh air, and cherry trees have brought parts of Sweetie back to me, and it's such a gift.

"I know," I reassure her. "It's for my benefit, so I don't have to worry. We're going to be walking a lot today, and the ground is uneven. I don't want you to fall."

The truth is, she's very unsteady on her feet as of late. She has to hold the furniture as she moves about the apartment. Her entire body seems to be breaking down before my eyes—mind and body, but not her spirit.

"There's my favorite lady," Abby's dad, William, greets us. "Why, hello, Ms. Sweetie."

Sweetie looks up from the wheelchair. "I'm sorry. Have we met?"

Abby's parents exchange subtle looks.

"I don't believe we have." William extends his hand out to Sweetie. "I'm William, one of the owners of this place. Welcome to the orchard."

"Nice to meet you," Sweetie says. "You do have quite a welcoming team here. Can't go wrong with good ole hospitality."

"We appreciate everyone who comes out to the orchard," William says. "Why don't you follow us, and we'll explain how everything works."

I've heard William's speech for new orchard goers a hundred times and could recite it myself if needed, but Sweetie seems to be fully invested in what he's saying, so we follow him as he explains how the cherry-picking process works. Plus, this is Hayes's first time. He should get the whole experience.

"And then when you're all done picking, bring up your bucket of cherries and we'll dump them into this machine here, which will pit them for you," he finishes and hands us all little cherry buckets.

"Thank you." I shoot him a smile before turning to Sweetie. "I think we're ready to pick. Let's go."

Hayes pushes Sweetie's wheelchair, and the two of them follow me out to the orchard.

"Hey, not to sound like a complete out-of-towner, but why do we need all of the cherries pitted? I mean, when you buy cherries in the store, they have pits," Hayes asks.

I turn back to face him. "The cherries in the cans have pits?"

"No, the fresh cherries that you get in the produce section," he clarifies.

"Oh, gotcha. That's because this orchard grows tart cherries. So these cherries are the ones that are dried or in the cans for pie fillings and desserts. Michigan produces seventy-five percent of the nation's tart cherries. We still produce about twenty percent of the nation's sweet cherries, but none of those orchards are around here. Most of them are a little south and along the coastline of Lake Michigan. All of the cherries we get today will be used for all sorts of baking, right Sweetie?" I look down at my grandmother.

She's zoned out, staring out toward the horizon.

I return my attention to Hayes. "Sweetie makes the best cherry cobbler, cherry chocolate chip bars, cherry cake, muffin, brownies...you name it, we have a recipe for it that includes cherries. I'll make a few of them, and then we'll freeze the rest."

"Sounds incredible. How do these cherries taste fresh?" He plucks a cherry off a tree.

"These are Montmorency cherries, which are perfect for canning, drying, and baking but not good for eating," I say as Hayes pops one into his mouth. "They are quite..."

"Sour." His face scrunches up.

"Yeah, definitely bitter," I release a quick laugh.

He spits out the seed and most of the cherry.

"I told you. They're baking cherries." I pick a handful off the tree and place them in the bucket on Sweetie's lap. "What should we make first?" I ask, rubbing the top of her hand with mine.

"What's that, dear?" She looks up at me, blinking a few times.

"I was asking what you want to make first with the cherries when we get back home?"

She tilts her head to the side, looking at something in the distance. "That sounds fine, dear."

I raise my gaze to Hayes to find a sad expression on his face. The corners of his mouth tilt up into a forced grin. "What's your favorite?" he asks me.

We continue down the rows of trees, picking as we go. "Probably the cobbler. The combination of the fruit, breading, and creamy vanilla ice cream is so good."

"You should make the cobbler first," he says.

I nod.

We pick cherries in silence. The sea of sadness that is my life is pulling me down. Submerging me. Forcing me to feel everything that I've been hiding from. What started out as such a promising day has only come to show me that Sweetie will never be the same. Our relationship, as I knew it, is gone. Forever. The most heartbreaking part is I don't even know when I lost her. I was trying so hard to hold on to her and everything she is to me that I didn't notice when she slipped away. I didn't say goodbye when she still knew me.

And now I'll never get the chance.

Her decline is not new, yet just moments ago, I had so much hope because she seemed different. We've picked cherries every year since I was born, and she and Pops picked them every year since they've been here. This orchard is a special part of our lives, and I was hoping the magic of nostalgia would bring her back for the day.

Just yesterday, I was filled with hope and joy, and now...

The back and forth of my emotions is only compounding my exhaustion.

Hayes's thumb wipes a tear from my cheek that I hadn't realized was there, bringing me back to the present. The small gesture is both comforting and startling. I release a clipped breath and take a step back.

"Sorry, I..."

What am I sorry for? For not being aware enough to realize when Sweetie and I had our last genuine moment? For trying so hard to do everything right but failing? For crying in the middle of an orchard with my—for all intents and purposes—business partner. For wanting him to hug me when I know it's not appropriate.

Maybe—all of the above.

Hayes steps toward me again. "Come here." He opens his arms.

I eye the invitation, and I'd be lying if I said I didn't want to fall against his chest, but I'm stronger than that.

"It's not...I'm...It's fine." My mind refuses to process the simple thought.

"It's just a hug, Evie. Between friends. I think you could use one." He takes another step, and this time, he wraps his arms around me. With a sigh, I give in and lean against him.

His strong arms pull me close, and the connection shatters my walls. The barriers I've relied on to give me strength crumble, and the tears come.

It's stupid really. Standing in the middle of my

friend's cherry orchard with strangers passing, Sweetie unaware of my breakdown, in the arms of a man I barely know—I completely fall apart. Tears stream down my face, and I let them fall, not that I have a choice. Realization dawns on me, and my heart shatters. Despair leaves me in waves.

"She's all I have, and I don't even have her anymore," I choke out between sobs. Hayes rubs my back and remains quiet while I cry.

After a few minutes, the tears subside, and I pull away, stepping back. "I'm sorry." I wipe the back of my hand across my face. "I guess it all just hit me. We do this every year, and today just made me realize how different everything is now. Just last year, cherry picking was a completely different experience. It's all happening so fast."

"I'm sorry you have to go through this," he says.

"Thanks. Me too." I look around. "Gosh, this is your first Cherry Blossom Grove picking experience, and I totally ruined it." I scrunch up my nose.

"No, you didn't."

"Yes, I did."

"You just made it more colorful." He walks back to Sweetie and starts to push her chair again.

"Well, that's another way to say it, I guess," I huff out a laugh. "Let's head back. We have plenty."

Hayes turns Sweetie's chair around, and we start back toward the barns.

"Um, Evie?" Hayes says, his voice hesitant.

"Yeah?"

"A giant pig is running toward us." His eyes dart from side to side as if he's looking for cover from an attack.

I laugh. "Don't worry. That's just Gloria. She won't hurt you."

Gloria, in her six hundred pounds of glory, stops when she reaches me, and I rub behind her ears. "Hello there, pretty girl." She snorts, and I pluck a cherry from a tree, pop out the seed, and give it to her. She swallows it and purses out her bottom lip, ready for more. So I give her another one.

Hayes watches with fascination as I feed Gloria.

"Hey, guys!" Abby waves. She's walking toward us, accompanied by her giant bullmastiff, Blue.

"Bluey!" I call, and Blue jogs toward me. I give him some neck rubs. Gloria nudges my arm for more cherries.

"Don't let her fool you. She's already eaten three times today." Abby chuckles. "Pa relieved me at the cash register so I could come say hi. I didn't see you when you got here. How's it going?" She directs the last question to Hayes.

"Good," he says, still focused on the pig.

"She's harmless. I promise." Abby notices Hayes's apprehension.

"So you have a pet pig?" he asks the obvious.

"Yeah, she's part of the family. Aren't ya, girl?" Abby pats Gloria on the rear. "Are you guys heading back?"

I nod. "We've gotten enough."

"Oh, good. I'll walk with you. So how's the transition of the shop going? I'm sorry I haven't been by. You know how it is here right now."

"I'd say it's going well." I look at Hayes.

"Great," he agrees. "About ready to finalize everything."

"Has it been a month already?" she asks.

"Almost." I nod. It's hard to believe that Hayes has been here for three weeks already. The time has flown by. "Hayes has a week left, and then we'll sign everything and transition ownership."

"Well, that's exciting." Abby picks up a stick from the ground and throws it. Blue runs after it.

"So, this is your place?" Hayes asks Abby.

"Someday. Right now, it still belongs to my parents, but eventually, I'll inherit it. It's been in my dad's family since the beginning."

"Abby's family helped found this town back over a hundred years ago. They settled here and started this orchard, and the town grew from there," I say to Hayes.

"Yep. That's true. Duncan Street, Mary Avenue, and William Street that run through downtown were all named after our family. Generations of Duncans have lived here."

"That's so cool," Hayes says. "It's one of my favorite things about this place—the stories. Evie has so many of them, as do all of the customers that come into the shop. Everyone knows everyone and has stories to prove it. It's fascinating and not something you find in large cities. It's just one of the things that make this place so special."

Abby takes the stick that Blue has retrieved from his mouth and throws it again. "It is really special. Granted, I don't have anything to compare it to as I've never lived anywhere else, but I love it here. I wouldn't trade my time here for anything."

"Me either," I agree. Abby squeezes my hand and then looks down toward Sweetie, who is nodding off.

"We better get your cherries over to the pitter and get you checked out," she says.

"Yeah," I agree. "Sweetie is definitely ready to go."

After our cherries are pitted and paid for, we pack up the car. Sweetie leans against the back of the seat, her eyes heavy with exhaustion. I close the door and walk around the back. Hayes shuts the trunk and stands before me.

"You know, you're wrong about one thing," he says.

"What?" I ask, confused.

"She's not all you have." It takes me a few seconds to realize what he's referring to. "You said that she was all you have, and she's not. I've only been here a few weeks, and I know that's not true at all. Everyone in this town loves you. You have more true, quality friends than most people have in a lifetime. You are loved, Evie Emberton, by many. I'm so sorry that you're losing your nana, but don't think for a second that you're alone."

I force a swallow and nod.

"You know that, right?" he presses.

"Yeah," I say, and despite my saddened heart, I know he's right. And for a brief moment, the weight on my shoulders feels a little less heavy.

Chapter Twenty-One

W e drive back to town in silence. So many emotions swirl within my mind. I'm trying to find the good in my situation with my nana. My grandparents always taught me to look for the good in everything because no matter how dark a situation may seem, there's always light. I was taught to focus on the light when life became difficult.

Goodness exists everywhere. Focusing on the light will pull you through the darkness faster. My grandfather's words fill my brain.

Thinking back to my pops' death, which was sudden, unexpected, and devastating, I wonder if Sweetie's situation where I know it's coming is easier. It's hard to tell. The grief of his death has been diluted by time and situation. It's no longer comparable to my present.

Throughout the past year of Sweetie's decline, her friends have come from everywhere to show their love.

Meals, visits, and laughs have been shared, and it's been heartwarming. I suppose for those friends these visits are part of their grieving process. They've been able to talk to Sweetie, knowing she is leaving us. That's a shred of light in the darkness.

I suppose I've had the same time, yet it's hard to be grateful for something that's been slowly stealing my nana away from me, piece by piece. Time is contributing to both the light and the darkness surrounding me.

This experience has led me down the path of a new career. Thanks to Hayes and his friendly conversations over breakfast at the B&B, I'm well on my way to becoming an established family photographer.

And Hayes...unexpectedly, he's been a shining light over the past few weeks. I've grown to crave his presence and need his help, which could also be filed away under both the good and the bad. I shouldn't want him around as much as I do because he'll be gone in a week.

I park the car, and Hayes helps me get Sweetie up the stairs and into the apartment. I make her a sandwich, and she eats half of it before stating that she's tired and going to bed. It's hours before she normally calls it a night, but today's extra excursion has wiped her out.

After she's tucked into bed, I find Hayes in the kitchen feeding Pumpkin.

He looks up from scooping the canned food onto a plate. "I hope this is okay. I know it sounds crazy, but he was insisting. He is extremely bossy."

I laugh, and it's refreshing. "He is the bossiest cat in

the world, and yeah...it's fine. Saves me from doing it because had you resisted his demands, he'd be shrieking at my feet right now." I watch Pumpkin devour his food with a smile on my face. I look at Hayes and find him watching me. I pull in a breath. "Thank you for everything today."

"No problem. While you were helping Sweetie, I went downstairs and let Aidan go home and closed up the store."

I bring my palm to my head. "The shop," I groan. "I had completely forgotten about it. How crazy is that? Thank you. Were there any gummies left?" I press my lips together in a grin.

"Yeah, surprisingly so. Though his girlfriend was hanging out with him behind the counter, and whatever was going on there didn't look too innocent." He raises a brow.

I wave my hand dismissively. "Eh, their parents can tackle that one. I can only take so much responsibility in one day." I open the refrigerator. "I'm going to warm up some ravioli from last night. Do you want some? I also have a quinoa salad."

"Ravioli sounds great. Thanks."

"Hazel dropped off some of her family's cherry wine, and it's fantastic."

Hayes opens the cupboard above the sink where I keep the wine and pulls out a bottle. I work on warming up the dinner, and he opens and pours the wine. Everything is so comfortable between us, and it gives me pause.

One week left.

We sit at the table with our leftover pasta and sweet wine.

"You know so many of my stories. Tell me some more of yours," I say, mainly because I'm interested, but also because I'm too exhausted to talk myself.

He finishes taking a sip of his wine and licks his lips, setting the wineglass down. "Okay." He nods, his face scrunches in thought before he says, "Would you like to hear about the time that I fell down the laundry chute?"

I let out a short laugh, knowing this story is going to be great. "First of all, explain what you mean by laundry chute. I want to make sure I'm picturing it correctly."

Hayes sets his fork down and lifts his hands to start telling the story. I love that he's a hand talker because I am too. Honestly, there are many things I love about him. "Well, our washer and dryer are in the basement, and our bedrooms are on the second level. Mom got tired of lugging hampers of dirty laundry down two flights of stairs, so my dad cut a square hole in the floor next to the toilet in the upstairs bathroom. Using this thin metal material, he built a chute that ran from the bathroom down through the walls and into the basement. Then we just tossed our dirty clothes in the chute, and they would slide down the tunnel and land on the floor in front of the washing machine."

"Oh my gosh, that is so cool."

"Yeah, my dad was always doing projects like that. Little improvements around the house that most wouldn't think of but ones that made life a little better. You know? So, anyway, when I was six, Hattie dared me to jump down the chute."

I cover my mouth. "Oh no." I giggle.

"Yeah." He raises a brow. "I did—of course, it was a dare—but there is a bend halfway down the tunnel that angles to the side to direct the clothes toward the washing machine, and I got stuck when my feet hit that bend. Plus, the thing was never intended for children to go through, so there were a few places with jagged metal exposed that would not be good if I slid by."

I stare at Hayes with bated breath. He's such a great storyteller.

"The other thing that I should mention was that Mom was nine months pregnant with Grace. She ran into the bathroom when Hattie started screaming for help and reached her hand into the chute to grab me. She was trying her hardest to pull me out but didn't have the strength. She held me as long as she could but was getting tired. So, she had Hattie grab a broom, and she laid it across the opening of the chute, and she and Hattie pulled me up until I could grab onto the broom handle. Then she ran to call my uncle, who thankfully only lived five minutes away. He came over and pulled me out."

"Oh my gosh." I laugh.

"I know." Hayes shakes his head. "I still hear about that move at family functions even now."

"Your poor mom, trying to hold you up with a giant belly." I grin. "I would love to meet Hattie and Grace. I bet they have so many stories about you."

"Oh, they do." He nods.

"Tell me another."

He looks at me, a squint to his big browns, and he nods as if he's just thought of another interesting tale to share.

Hayes launches into another story, and I listen, sipping my wine. I get lost in his words and memories, and I want to stay there.

Two bottles of cherry wine and many stories later, Hayes's gaze captures mine, and it morphs from light-hearted to serious in an instant.

I clear my throat. "What is it?"

He bends his head and rubs the back of his neck before raising his stare. "I have to tell you something."

"Okay," I urge.

"Well, there's this family-owned chain we're buying out. The main store is in a little town in Maine, but he has a handful of stores located down the coast. It's a pretty profitable business and is going to be a big contract for my company. So my bosses want me on location in Maine until the sale is finalized to make sure everything runs smoothly."

"When?"

"I leave tomorrow." He presses his lips together in a line.

"Tomorrow?" There's more of a screech to my voice than I'm comfortable with.

"Yeah. The owner is ready to start negotiations, and I have to be there for that. I don't see it being an in and out deal like Key West was. I'll probably be there a week."

"You still had a week of your month left here?"

"I know, but truthfully, I have everything I need. I've already submitted the training protocol for the new manager and employees. My boss is happy with everything and thinks it's time for me to go elsewhere. Rhonda, my assistant, will fly in with the final paperwork at the end of the week, and you'll be done and free to do whatever makes you happy." His words are cheerful, but I hear a sense of sadness in them, too. At least I hope I do.

I want to hear the sorrow in his voice because the words he just spoke unleashed visceral grief within me that I don't have the right to feel. This has always been the plan. He was going to learn how to run the business effectively and leave. I always thought a month was too long for what he needed to accomplish. This makes sense. Of course, he's ready to move on.

One more week with Hayes wouldn't have changed the result, yet I'm devastated that he's leaving early. Time is one of the most precious commodities, and he just stole seven days from me. An entire week of minutes that I needed. And that's the thing—I've grown to need Hayes, and that mistake is on me. I knew better. I felt my feelings for him evolving, and I didn't stop them. I let this happen when he was always meant to leave.

I want to fight for him, beg him to stay, tell him that I need him, but I can't. My feelings were never part of the plan.

"Okay," I force out the two-syllable word, and it feels like a lie as it leaves my lips.

"You're okay?"

"Yeah, of course." Another lie.

I won't betray myself anymore. I don't need Hayes, I have myself, and there isn't anything that I can't do. His friendship became a security blanket that made me weak, and I have to be strong for Sweetie and me. Security blankets are a false sense of control. They can be ripped away at any moment, and one is left with only themselves. I have to be enough.

I stand from the table, taking a handful of dirty dishes with me. "Well, it's late."

"Evie." Hayes pleads for a peek into my thoughts, but I'm done giving myself away.

"I'm tired. Just ready for bed." I smile weakly.

He follows me into the kitchen with his plates and sets them in the sink. "Can I help you clean up?"

I shake my head. "No, you should go. I'll finish this up in the morning."

"Okay." He bows his head. "Well, my flight leaves really early, so this is goodbye, then."

"Yeah, I guess it is." I follow him to the door.

He opens the door and turns to face me. "I've had a wonderful time here in Cherry Blossom Grove. I want to thank you for everything."

"No problem. Best of luck with all your business buying." It's a lame goodbye, but it's what I have.

"Thanks." He leans against the doorframe and captures my gaze. "I'm going to miss you, Evie Emberton."

I blow out a breath and shrug, forcing a grin. "I am easy to miss."

My heart races as he leans in and places his lips against my cheek. He gives me a quick kiss, and then he leaves.

I watch until he disappears down the stairs, and I shut the door, locking the deadbolt. I lean my back against the door and slide down until I'm seated on the floor.

And then I cry.

Chapter Twenty-Two

I bring the mug to my lips and take a long sip of coffee. It's liquid heaven for my soul. I think back to my childhood. I always found it weird that Pops and Sweetie loved coffee as much as they did. Brewing a pot was always the first thing they did upon waking, and as a child, I thought it was silly. I tried my grandfather's coffee once and remembered thinking that it was highly overrated. I told myself that I would grow up to be a non-coffee drinker. That thought was the height of my rebellious stage.

I don't know when it happened. It was gradual, and I can't pinpoint when, but at some point, I was a deep admirer of the warm liquid made from magic beans. And it is magic. I won't start my day without it.

Today, especially, I need the fortifying strength that coffee brings. Hayes left this morning, and I'm having a tough time processing the emptiness within my heart. He said goodbye last night, and despite having not even spent a day without him yet, I miss him. Just knowing he's gone is torture. The whole thing is ridiculous. I've known him for three weeks. When all is said and done, his presence will fill less than a chapter in the book of my life. However, there's this feeling within me that I could've written an entire book just about him—if I had the chance.

"I was thinking about taking Ms. Sweetie to the library today. They are having a craft day to kick off the cherry festival. Do you think she'd like that?" Christine asks.

I focus my thoughts on the present, locking musings of coffee and Hayes away. "Yeah, I do. One of the volunteers there, Betty, is an old classmate of Sweetie's. She might remember her. She has an easier time remembering people she's known for decades." I tip the mug up and gulp down the rest of my coffee. "Thank you for thinking of doing that. I hate that she spends so much time in the apartment."

"No problem. It will be fun."

I quickly brush my teeth again because as much as I love coffee, I'm not a fan of coffee breath. After exiting the bathroom, I open Sweetie's bedroom door and peek in. She's still sleeping. I blow her a silent kiss before heading out.

"Well, I'm going to make my way down to the shop.

Please don't hesitate to call me if you need anything," I tell Christine.

"Will do."

The shop seems lonelier today with the knowledge that Hayes isn't going to walk through that door any minute.

Enough, I tell myself.

I unlock the front door and turn on the multicolored open sign hanging in the front window. I step out of the shop and stand on the sidewalk. The air is warm and sweet. A plump robin pecks at the base of the tree in front of me, and I quickly make a wish. When I was younger, I was told to always make a wish on the first robin of spring that I see. Somehow, that has turned into making a wish every time I see the orange-bellied bird.

Peace is what I wish for. I simply want to feel that I'm doing the right thing for Sweetie and me. It's been such a whirlwind as of late, and sometimes I feel swept up in all of the change. I start to question things but never find solid answers. And maybe that's not how life works. Perhaps, I'll never know for certain if all the decisions I've made are the right ones. But I hope I can find peace with them.

"Good morning, Evie," Mrs. Fredericks says as she passes by on the way to her morning stop at the bakery.

"Good Morning, Mrs. Fredericks. Tell Cal I said hi."

"I sure will, doll."

Lacey Ann waves to me from across the street, and I

wave back. Someone honks in greeting as they pass, and I wave even though I'm not sure who it was. I can see the shop owners across the street preparing their stores for the day through the front windows.

I smile. It's going to be a lovely day.

Stepping back into the shop, Pumpkin lays across the top of the glass jelly bean containers.

"Get down from there," I tell him. "You know we're going to have to lock up your kitty door for good in another week. You're not going to be able to come down here anymore."

With that thought, I walk over to him and pet him instead of shooing him off the containers. They're sealed, so it's fine. Plus, I don't have the heart to deny him when he only has a week left in this place.

The bell above the door chimes and I turn to find Hazel walking through the door.

"Hey, girl," she greets me.

"Good morning." I grin. "What are you doing here so early?"

"Well, I got a text from Abby, who got a text from Audrey that Hayes left for good. I wanted to check on you. Are you okay? What happened? Why did he leave early?"

I shake my head with a chuckle. Another perk of small-town living is that everyone knows everyone's business and, as in this case, often in record speed.

"Well, he has a big deal in Maine that he needs to close, and his boss wanted him there. So he left." I shrug.

"And?" She eyes me expectantly.

"And what? I'm fine."

She raises a brow. "I don't buy it."

"What?" I roll my eyes playfully and walk over to the counter, where I take a seat.

Hazel follows me. "You like him. I know you do."

"I like him as a person, sure. He became a good friend, but his time here always had an expiration date, Hazel. What do you want me to say?"

"I don't know. I just saw something between you two when you were together. It seemed like more."

I raise my shoulders. "Maybe there was. Maybe there wasn't. Either way, it doesn't matter, though, because he left. His company is sending in some woman with the paperwork this weekend, and then I'll sign, and it will be done. My days will be spent with Sweetie and photography. I can spend more time with you all. It will be good," I say as much to convince myself as Hazel.

"You're right." She sighs. "If he left...I guess it doesn't matter anymore. I just thought he was different."

Pumpkin hurls his large frame up onto the counter and plops down in front of Hazel. She pets him, and he starts to purr.

"What do you mean?" I ask.

"I saw the way he looked at you, Evie. You know I'm good at reading people. I honestly didn't think he would leave. It's naïve, I suppose. I just felt he would stay."

I bite my lip. "Yeah, I guess a part of me did too."

"Well"—Hazel claps her hands together—"that is that. Let's drink to new beginnings."

"Drink?"

"Yeah, with root beer of course." She winks and walks over to the cooler and fills two small cups with the brown soda.

She hands a cup to me and holds out her own. I extend my arm out to press my cup against hers. "To new beginnings and exciting new adventures," she says.

"Cheers," I say, and we tap our cups together and take a drink.

She taps her lips with her forefinger. "Now that you're not going to be working all of the time, I need to think about who I should set you up with in town."

I laugh. "I think I'll pass. How about we talk about you? What's going on with you and Cal?"

"Nothing. It's just a flirtation thing, really. It's been too many years of back and forth to be anything serious at this point, you know? Oh, what about Eli?"

"What about Eli?" I ask.

"For you. I mean, you liked him in high school. Any chance that romance needs to be rekindled?" She looks hopeful.

"No." I grin. "We're just friends, and stop with the matchmaker stuff. I don't need a boyfriend right now. I have enough going on in my life."

"Fine," Hazel groans. "But once you get settled into your new routine after the sale of the shop is final, I'm setting you up with someone."

"We'll talk about that then," I say to placate her.

The door to the shop opens, and Cal walks in with a white box. "I come bearing gifts." He places the cardboard box onto the counter next to Pumpkin and opens the lid to reveal an amazing selection of donuts.

"Yum." I look at him. "What is all of this for?"

"I just saw Mrs. Fredericks, and she said that you were feeling down because Hayes left today so I thought I'd bring some goodies over to cheer you up."

"What?" I scoff. "How does Mrs. Fredericks know that Hayes left? And I do not need cheering up." I laugh. "You guys, I'm fine."

"So you don't want the donuts?" He smirks.

"Oh, I definitely want them." I pull the box toward me.

"Me too." Hazel reaches in and grabs a cherry fritter.

I take a soft glazed donut. They are my favorite, simple and delicious. "Thank you, Cal," I say.

"You're welcome." He reaches his hand out to pet Pumpkin. "What are you ladies up to this morning?"

"We're talking about boys." Hazel puts an emphasis on the last word.

Cal's eyes go wide. "All right. Well, I can't stay. Just wanted to check in on you, Evie. Have a great day," he says to Hazel and me before leaving as quickly as he came.

I take a bite of my donut. "You're mean," I say with a giggle.

Hazel puckers her lips. "What? It's true."

I take another sip of the root beer, which, surprisingly enough, accompanies donuts pretty well, and I feel happy.

Hayes was right.

I'm not even close to being alone.

Chapter Twenty-Three

I pull the last pink foam roller out of Sweetie's hair and place it in the box. She's had this same container of curlers ever since I can remember. This is my first attempt at styling her hair the way she used to. I've watched her do it more times than I can count, so I hope I can pull it off.

She's quiet as I brush her curls into place, fashioning them into the wavy bob style that she used to wear for all special occasions. And today is definitely that.

It's our grand send-off downstairs in the shop. A final party to celebrate all that *Sweet as Pie* has meant to my family and the community before I hand over ownership.

It's hard to believe that just a month ago, I decided to sell the family business. The past thirty days have flown by, yet so much has happened. I can't explain it, but I've changed. I'm not the desperate girl I was a month ago. I'm more confident in my skin and with my decisions. My life is still as chaotic as ever, but I'm content.

I stare at Sweetie's reflection in the mirror. She seems to be zoned out and lost in her own world. Her expression is vacant. Her face carries more wrinkles than it did even a month ago. Age is swallowing her up at a rapid speed. Yet for all the new lines on her face, she's still as beautiful as ever. I've always been told that my mother was the spitting image of Sweetie and that I look just like my mother. I hope to be as elegant as Sweetie is when I reach this age.

"I think your hair is complete," I say. "How does it look?"

She focuses on the mirror before her but doesn't say a word.

"How about some lipstick?" I retrieve her favorite shade from the makeup bag and hold it up for her approval. When she doesn't protest, I apply it to her lips.

"There," I say. "Now, you're ready for the party."

Sweetie allows me to help her into the living room. She's been exceedingly quiet the last week but not frightened, at least from what I can tell.

"Well, don't you look lovely," Christine, the nurse, says to Sweetie.

"Yes, she does. She is the guest of honor tonight, after all." I smile toward Sweetie before addressing Christine. "Can you please just give me a minute, and then we'll head down."

"Of course, take your time." Christine slides her arm through Sweetie's and leads her toward a chair.

I hurry toward my bedroom and take a quick look at myself in the mirror. I'm not sure what one should wear to a company goodbye party, but a little black dress is never wrong. My long red hair is down and in loose waves instead of its usual ponytail, and it looks good. I applied minimal makeup and lipstick but enough to highlight my features. Hazel would be proud. My reflection is one of confidence and class.

I got this, I nod to myself in the mirror.

I snatch the black bowtie collar off my dresser and approach Pumpkin, who lays sprawled on my bed. "A goodbye party wouldn't be complete without you. Please don't protest," I plead as I place the collar around his neck. To my surprise, he allows it with little more than a groan. "Oh, my goodness. You look so adorable. And look, we match."

The orange fluff ball isn't impressed. I swing the strap of my camera bag over my shoulder before picking Pumpkin up. Exiting my room, I let Christine know that we're ready, and the four of us head down to the shop.

The space is decked out with dozen of balloons in all different colors. I've set up a table with a variety of sweet treats for the partygoers to help themselves too. White twinkle lights hang around the perimeter of the room where the walls meet the ceiling. The party theme is happy. Everything in this room makes me think of happiness, from the lights to the colors to the sweets. Yet what makes me the most joyous is already standing outside the shop window waiting for the party, and that's the people.

I set Pumpkin down on the counter, along with my camera, and help Christine get Sweetie situated in her chair. With one final look around to make sure everything is ready, I unlock the front door.

"Evie!" I'm met with boisterous greetings and hugs as people enter.

"Welcome! Welcome," I say as everyone walks through the door.

The party was announced as an open house with a timeframe of four hours for people to stop by, and it wasn't scheduled to start for another fifteen minutes, yet the shop is already full of smiling faces here to support Sweetie and me. My heart swells with so much joy.

"This is for you," a teen girl named Everly says as she hands me a gift bag. Her parents stand behind her, wearing large grins.

"Thank you so much," I tell her.

"Open it," she says, eagerly.

"Well, okay then." I chuckle and pull out a little professionally bound scrapbook. There's a picture of me, Sweetie, and Pops on the cover with the name of the shop that must have been taken about a year before Pops died.

"That picture was taken on my third birthday," she says, pointing at the cover of the book. I run my finger over the glossy cover and the picture of my grandparents.

Opening the book, I find a baby Everly that I barely remember staring back at me. "That was my first birthday," she says, and I turn the page. "And my second." There's a collage of shots of two-year-old Everly with a birthday tiara on her head and the candy displays behind her. "My parents have brought me here every year on my birthday since the very first one. It's my favorite place and my birthday tradition."

My eyes fill with tears as I look through the remainder of the book. "Oh my gosh, I love this so much." I hold the book to my chest. "Thank you for making this for me. I will always cherish it."

"We sure are going to miss you," Everly's dad says.

"It won't be the same without one of the Embertons here to greet us," Everly's mom says. "I've been coming here for my birthdays since I was a kid as well."

"That's incredible. Thank you so much for coming in all of these years. I'm going to miss being here, too," I tell them. They each give me a hug, and I thank them again for their thoughtful gift before they head over to where Sweetie is sitting. I place the scrapbook back into the gift bag and put it on the back counter.

Pumpkin lays across the glass display as two kids pet him and giggle over his bow tie.

"Evie." I turn to find Mrs. McNeely, a longtime friend of the family, standing behind me with a beautifully wrapped gift. She extends the package for me, and I take it. "Just a little something for you and your next new adventure."

"Mrs. McNeely, you didn't have to get me anything," I say.

She waves her hand. "Oh, it was no trouble. You can open it later. I simply wanted to let you know that I think so highly of you, and I adore you, just as I've always adored your family. I am here for you if you ever need anything. It's a shame that you're selling the shop, but I sure do hope you find everything that you're looking for."

"Thank you. That means a lot." I set the gift next to my other one. "Can I get you a complimentary root beer float?" I ask.

"You know. I've been trying to cut down on my sugar intake as of late, but it's a celebration, is it not? So, I think I will have a root beer float. Thank you." She grins.

"Well, you know what they say?" I scoop some ice cream into a cup. "The sugar doesn't count if it's a celebration." I shoot her a wink as I pour the soda over the ice cream and hand it to her.

"I think you're right. Thank you, dear."

"Thank you for coming, Mrs. McNeely."

Person after person come up to me. Hugs are given. Stories are shared. The counter fills with gifts, cards, and mementos of thanks from the townspeople. Each person who greets me has a beautiful story of what this shop or my family means to them. Many of the stories are old favorites of mine, but there's a good number I've never heard before.

Mrs. Wright, one of our regular customers, stands

before me, grasping my hands in hers. "Do you remember that carnival-themed weekend that Sweetie and Pops organized when you were about twelve?" she asks me.

"Yes, I do because Pops rented a cotton candy machine, and I thought it was incredible." I think back to that weekend. We've had many themed events over the years, but I was especially fond of that one because of the cotton candy.

"Well, that was right after my husband Bill passed away, and you couldn't have known, but I was very close to losing our house. The medical bills and cost of the funeral had taken what savings we had. I was a stay-at-home mother and needed time to find work. I thought I was going to lose everything." Her eyes fill with tears. "Your grandparents organized that event to raise money for my family. They gave me every cent they made that weekend, and it was enough to cover our bills for a couple of months while I found employment. They saved my family."

I press my palm against my chest. "I had no idea."

"No one did, and in this town, that's something. You know how the gossip mill is here. That's the thing about your grandparents. They were incredible people, and they did things to help others out of the kindness of their hearts, not because they wanted recognition. Of course, I thanked them many times over the years because they truly saved us and allowed me to keep a roof over my children's heads. My children had lost their father, and

Sweetie and Pops made sure they didn't lose their home, too. I could never repay them. But I wanted to tell you because you should know how incredible Pops and Sweetie were, and how you are just like them."

I wipe a tear from my cheek. "I know how special they are, but I appreciate you telling me your story. That means so much to me. I could never live up to them, but I try."

She shakes her head. "You do more than try, sweet girl. You are just like them."

I look over at Sweetie, who sits quietly as one of her friends speaks to her. She wears a blank expression.

Mrs. Wright sighs, following my stare. "I miss her, too. Just know that wherever she is, she's so proud of you."

I pull my attention from Sweetie. "Thank you," I tell Mrs. Wright. She gives me a hug before leaving me to mingle with some of the other people at the party.

"Oh my gosh, finally!" Abby squeals and pulls me into a hug. "We've been trying to talk to you for like an hour. You're a hard one to get to tonight." Hazel, Matty, Aubrey, Cal, and Eli stand behind Abby, and each come in for an embrace.

"Hi, guys! Thanks for coming," I tell my friends.

"Like we would miss it." Hazel hands me a gift bag with several bottles of wine.

I take the bag from Hazel, and one from Abby and Aubrey, too. "Why is everyone bringing me gifts, tonight?" I laugh. "This is so weird."

"We're celebrating you," Aubrey exclaims. "Of course, we'd bring gifts."

I place the presents next to the other ones. "It's just so overwhelming. All of the gifts, and stories, and so many kind words from everyone. I didn't expect it, I guess. At least not so much of it. It's humbling."

"Everyone is going to miss you," Cal says. "And by the way, you look beautiful."

"Agreed, absolutely gorgeous," Abby chimes in.

"Thank you. And I appreciate all of the kindness and support, but I'm not going anywhere." I shake my head.

Abby looks around, "I know, but it's an end of an era, and people will miss seeing you here. Despite how great Hayes's report and training plan is, no one can replace you. It won't be the same."

"Yeah, I suppose," I respond.

"Speaking of Hayes, have you heard from him?" Aubrey asks.

I shake my head. "No, not since he left the apartment Monday night."

Honestly, I don't want to think about Hayes tonight. I've thought about him more than I should have throughout the week. Tonight is about my family and our shop. It's about thanking the community for supporting us all of these years. I'll have tomorrow to miss Hayes again, but I won't go there today.

I look at my group of friends. The way they've huddled around me has blocked me off from the rest of the party, giving me a reprieve from greeting guests. "Hey, I've been wanting to take pictures of everyone at the party to make into a scrapbook later but haven't had a second. Do you guys mind if I slip away for a minute?"

"Not at all. Go for it," Eli says.

"Awesome. We can chat in a bit. Go make yourself some floats or grab some food," I offer.

Abby rubs her belly. "Oh, we've definitely been eating."

"Okay." I laugh. "Well, I'll be back."

I sneak behind the counter and pull my camera out of my bag. Turning it on, I bring it to my face. Like the shield that my friends provided, the camera will do the same. It's not that I don't want to talk to everyone here, I do, but I want to capture the party as well.

I start clicking, taking photos of everyone at the party. There's a sea of faces, more than have ever been in this space at once. I snap shots of people, both young and old, partaking in the goodies. Laughter bounces off the walls, filling all the space within as neighbors reminisce and children climb under the tables with hands full of candy. This place has always done that. It's always brought people together and made them smile. Many friends have told me tonight that no matter what they were feeling when they walked through the shop's doors, they would always leave feeling lighter, happier.

This place is magical. Pops and Sweetie made it so. Sweet treats ignite the joy, but the space of love and light that my grandparents created brings the joy to life. It's special. Looking through the lens of my camera, I can see it on everyone's faces.

The smiles.

The laughter.

The embraces.

The community.

Sweet as Pie is so much more than a candy shop. It's a beating heart inside of this beautiful community of souls. I feel like I've known this, yet I'm realizing it for the very first time. What my grandparents created matters. What I do matters.

There's no way I can let this go.

Chapter Twenty-Four

Realization dawns and hits me with incredible force. Suddenly, the questions that I've been asking have all been answered. This place isn't a burden; it's a gift. To be able to be an important part in someone's life, to bring someone joy, help a friend, or celebrate with a neighbor is a blessing.

I slowly lower the camera from my face and look around in awe at all of these people in this room. I can't give this up. I always thought that I needed to sell this place to make my own way in life, but this is my way. This is my legacy. I've chosen to work open to close, every day, for years. I could've easily hired someone to give me a break. With the addition of an employee, I can still have a photography business. I can do both. Hiring someone to help me consistently will also give me more time with Sweetie. Someday, my grandmother won't be here, but a part of her will always live on through me and the community of love she created here, just as my Pops lives on through it now.

I used to believe I worked at the shop for my grandparents, but now I know that I work here for me. That simple switch in mentality is everything. A month ago, I stopped listening to my gut, and I tried to rationalize everything and overthought it all. Sweetie always told me to listen to my gut because it will never steer me wrong. The unease I've been feeling these past weeks has been my body telling me that I'm making the wrong choice.

I wasn't listening, but I am now. *I'm not selling.*

I kick off my heels and climb onto a chair so I can see everyone. Hazel notices my stance and whistles loudly. The chatter in the room ceases, and all heads turn toward me.

"Hi," I wave toward the crowded room. The sea of faces blur together, but I search for the one I need to see. I find Sweetie staring up at me, and I smile down at her. I pull in a steady breath and swallow the emotion in my throat.

"First, I wanted to thank you all for coming. I have loved speaking with you tonight and hearing your stories. You all know how much I adore everyone in this community. Cherry Blossom Grove is an incredible place to live full of amazing people, um..." My lip trembles as tears come to my eyes.

"Take your time, dear," someone cheers me on.

"Thank you." I chuckle and wipe the tears from my

cheeks. "I guess I'm just overcome with emotion because tonight has reminded me what's important. As you all know, this has been a very difficult year for us." I glance toward Sweetie. "And I wanted to do the right thing by everyone. I felt pulled in several directions and thought the answer was to sell this place, but now I realize that selling is the last thing I want to do."

A hushed murmur comes over the crowd.

"So, I guess what I'm trying to say is, I'm not selling!" I raise my arms in the air, and a deafening cheer erupts. Bringing my arms down, I clasp my hands together in front of my chest, and my lips turn up in the biggest smile.

After a minute of cheers, I say, "I'm sorry you all brought me goodbye presents. You can take them back if you want." I chuckle.

"Oh, you keep 'em, honey! You deserve it," a woman shouts.

"Well, I guess instead of a goodbye party, this is now an 'I'm here to stay' party," I exclaim as more hoots and hollers sound off. "I'll figure out what to do with the company scheduled to buy the place tomorrow, but tonight, we celebrate." I raise an arm to more cheers. My head falls back in laughter, and I feel like a rock star.

I jump down from the stool and am instantly enveloped in hugs.

"Oh my gosh!" Abby squeals. "This is so exciting!"

"I'm so happy for you!" Hazel proclaims.

"Incredible!" Aubrey adds.

Matty pulls me up into his arms and spins me around. "You made the right call," he says as I laugh.

"Thank you!" I tell them all. "It feels right."

"Then it is," Cal agrees.

"I'd have to agree," a husky voice says from behind me. I freeze as the familiar timbre continues. "It's right, Evie."

I slowly spin around. Standing before me is the person I've been pretending not to think about for the past week with his perfectly disheveled chocolate locks and intoxicating brown eyes. I've imagined his face more times than I'd like to admit, yet my imagination didn't do him justice. Hayes in real life is so much more.

"What are you doing here?" I ask in astonishment. "When did you get here?"

"I came to give you a wish." He smiles down at me, and it does something crazy to my insides.

"What?" I ask just as I notice the bouquet of licorice sticks in his hand.

I gasp, bringing my hands to my face. The long red sticks are tied together with a purple satin bow. He extends the candy bouquet toward me, and I wrap my fingers around the ribbon.

I raise my eyes to Hayes, and he captures my gaze in his. The rest of the room fades away, and it's just him and me, separated by a pile of licorice sticks.

"It's like when my...you remembered." I swallow hard, my eyes filling with unshed tears.

"I remember everything you've told me," he states.

"Why are you here? Did you come back with the sale paperwork?"

"No. I came back for you."

"I don't understand," I whisper.

He takes one of my hands in his, and the heat of his grasp sends chills down my spine. My other hand clings to the licorice bouquet like a lifeline.

"Leaving here, leaving you, was the worst I've ever felt. My time here with you changed me. I came here wanting to make a sale and left simply wanting you. During the time we spent together, I became enamored with your kindness, your wit, and your heart. You are the most beautiful person I've ever met, and as stunning as you are on the outside, you're even more incredible on the inside."

My heart is pounding so loudly, the beats are vibrating throughout my limbs and echoing in my ears, making me doubt everything I just heard.

Hayes continues. "I went to Maine questioning everything, especially the job I thought I loved. I no longer craved traveling all over the country to close on deals. I suddenly only wanted to be here in this three-stoplight town, where the people worship a small red fruit, selling candy next to you. I should've said something when I was here, but I wasn't completely convinced until I left. Like you, it took the prospect of losing something to realize what's important. Five days without you has shown me that I never want to spend another day without you again."

His words fuel my soul, and my body hums with the possibility of more.

"Really?" I swallow hard, the question is but a whisper.

"Really." His response is strong and solid, making me want to believe.

I look at Hayes and allow all of the emotions I've been keeping at bay to enter. And the truth is, there's an enormity of them. I, too, fell for Hayes as we worked side by side for those weeks. I was terrified of admitting it, but now that he's here and saying these things, the fear is gone.

The plethora of words that I want to say to him is bouncing around my mind like in a pinball machine. Overcome with emotion, I'm finding it difficult to settle my thoughts into coherent sentences to tell Hayes just how much he means to me and how incredibly grateful I am that he came back. So, I don't tell him with words, just yet. Instead, I stand on my tiptoes, throw my arms around his neck, and kiss him.

Cheers explode all around us. I pull my face away from Hayes's, and his giant smile mirrors my own. He wraps his arms around my middle and hugs me tight. I lean into his chest, and for the first time in a very long time, I feel completely at ease.

Hayes releases me from our hug.

"Find the short one and make a wish." He nods toward the candy bouquet still in my grasp.

The licorice pieces are starting to flop to the side.

I shake my head. "No. I don't need a wish. I have everything I need in this room."

I squeeze Hayes's hand, a silent *thank you* for everything he's done for me but mainly for coming back. I pivot to the side and walk toward Sweetie. Bending down, my face at her level, I hand her the licorice bouquet.

"Make a wish, Sweetie." I hold the bouquet out to her, and she takes it.

She stares at it with intensity for a moment and blinks a few times, seemingly confused, then she raises her gaze to find mine with a clarity I barely recognize anymore. "Evie?"

"Sweetie?" I gasp and hug her tight. "You're here."

"Darling." Her palm cradles my face. "My only wish is for your happiness."

"I am happy. I'm keeping the shop forever. And Hayes came back, and all of our friends are here to celebrate with us," I say quickly, uncertain of how long I have with her.

Tears stream down my face as Sweetie smiles at my words, a real genuine smile, and it fills my heart with so much gratitude that I'm sure it will burst.

"God willing, I'll meet your pops in heaven soon. Don't be sad for me. I've had a beautiful life. I love you, Evie girl."

I wrap my arms around her and rest my face against her beating heart. "I love you. I love you. I love you," I repeat the words over and over, allowing them to fill her soul so when she leaves, she'll carry my love with her.

Pumpkin jumps up on the chair, his fluff sticking to my wet cheeks. I sit back and look at my grandmother, but I'm only met with a vacant stare.

Just like that, she's gone.

I was just given a gift—her presence, borrowed time, sentiments of love—a goodbye. And it was my farewell. Deep in my heart, I'm certain that Sweetie won't be coming back again.

Chapter Twenty-Five

Small white Christmas lights are strung around the ceiling's perimeter, remnants of last night's party, creating fairy-like magic within the shop. The tiny beams of happiness shine from the hung strands and bounce off the glass candy cases, creating a rippling effect of twinkling dancing lights.

"Magic," I whisper to myself.

My grandfather started this place decades ago with next to nothing. It started small, only a few candies available at the beginning, but people came anyway. They came for the smiles and friendly conversations. They came for the feeling one gets when they step into these doors.

Regardless of what life stressors exist outside these walls, once people enter, all of it is forgotten—if only for a bit. Inside *Sweet as Pie* it's nostalgia, laughter, and sweets. Pops always said that candy won't change the world, but it can make everyone's world a little brighter, a little lighter, a little sweeter. He was so right. It's catching up with an old friend. It's spending one's allowance on Tootsie Rolls and having them taste like the best Tootsie Rolls in the world because they were earned. It's reminiscing over a root beer float. It's buying M&M's for your love on your anniversary because you ate them twenty years ago on your first date.

It's a special place, and it's mine.

On top of the counter by the cash register is a Mason jar filled with the licorice bouquet Hayes brought me last night. The red sticks are falling to the side, drooping over the edges of the jar like a sugary weeping willow. The sight of it makes me smile.

"It's looking a little sad today." Hayes chuckles, coming out of the storage room.

I tilt my head. "I don't know. I still like it." I motion to the shop. "Did you clean everything up?"

I expected to come downstairs to a mess this morning. Shortly after my emotional goodbye with Sweetie last night, Christine and I took her upstairs to bed. After she was tucked in and asleep, a wave of exhaustion hit me. It had been a tiring week with missing Hayes, preparing to hand over the shop, planning the goodbye open house, and then all of the emotions of the party. I physically only had enough energy to shoot a few people a text, asking them to lock up when everyone left. It's quite possible that I was asleep before my head hit my pillow. I knew everyone would understand.

Finding this place in pristine condition was a surprise.

"Your friends helped me clean most of it up last night, and then I finished up this morning," Hayes says.

"Well, thank you. That's so nice, and so appreciated."

Hayes walks over and pulls me into a hug. His warm embrace engulfs me, and I sigh against his chest.

"I'm so glad you're here," I tell him.

"Me too."

I take a step back. "So, tell me everything. What happened? When did you decide to come back? Did you quit your job? What did your boss say? Your family?" My questions come out at rapid speed, causing Hayes to laugh.

"I pretty much knew the second I left that I had to come back, honestly. I landed in Maine and called my boss to put in my notice. He offered me a remote position that I could do from here for as long as I want, and it doesn't require travel. Then I closed the deal in Maine and flew back. My family was surprised but supportive. They want me to be happy."

"So you're really here for good?" I still can't believe it.

"I really am."

"Did you know about the open house? Or was that a coincidence?"

"I knew. Aubrey told me."

"Of course she did." I shake my head with a chuckle.

Hayes shrugs. "Yeah, it helped having an inside informant. I mean, if I was going to come back and win my girl back, I wanted to do it in style." He puckers his lips into a cute smirk.

"Win me back?" I scoff. "You know we weren't a couple before."

"Not technically, but in all the ways that mattered, we were."

I squint my eyes. "Maybe."

"You know we were." He grins wide.

"I will say that you were pretty confident changing your job and coming in here, assuming that I would want something more." I quirk a brow.

Hayes's face turns serious. "When you know, you know. I felt it in here." He holds his hand to his heart. "I knew it was right. You hold my heart. There is no one else for me."

An overwhelming sense of déjà vu comes over me as I remember my pops speaking similar words.

"Did I say something wrong?" Hayes asks, concerned.

"No." I grin, wiping my tears. "Something right. My pops said almost those exact words about Sweetie once. These are happy tears."

"Come here." He pulls me into another hug.

I wrap my arms around his waist and breathe him in. I can't believe this day has come. The day, as my pops would say, I'd find the holder of my heart. Part of me worried that I was broken. I was afraid that maybe not everyone is meant to find their person, and that I wouldn't be as lucky in love as my grandparents were. I was wrong, so very wrong. The way I feel for Hayes is everything I've ever wanted.

Awareness hits as I realize that I have no idea where Hayes stayed last night.

I drop my arms and take a step back so I can see his face. "Where are you staying?"

"Aubrey had a room available at the B&B last night, so I stayed there."

"I'm so sorry." I press my palm to my head. "I wasn't even thinking. You showed up yesterday and said all of those amazing things, and then I just disappeared and left you to clean this place. Yesterday was so emotional, and I was drained. Have you ever been so tired that you just had to go to bed immediately?"

"Yes." He swipes a lock of hair that has fallen from my ponytail behind my ear. "It's fine. I get it. And I wanted to help clean up."

"You're so sweet." I squeeze his hand. "You should stay with us upstairs."

"Are you sure? I'm fine staying at the B&B."

I shake my head. "No, I insist. You're going to be here all of the time anyway, and I want to spend as much time with you as I can. It doesn't make sense to have you pay to stay at the B&B if you're barely there."

"Okay, if you're sure."

"I am. Glad that's settled. Also, did you know that I was going to pull out of the sale? I mean, wasn't

Rhonda supposed to be here an hour ago with the paperwork?"

Hayes nods. "Yeah, truthfully, I thought you'd pull out of the sale my first couple of days here."

"You did?" I laugh.

"Absolutely, I knew you wouldn't sell this place. It's part of who you are. It's your legacy, and it will always allow you to feel close to your grandparents. I think you were just overwhelmed and thought that selling was your only option."

"Why didn't you say something?" I raise a brow. "Instead, you just let me 'teach'"—I raise my hands in air quotes—"you all about the place."

"Why do you think? Because I wanted to spend time with you," Hayes grins. "If I convinced you of what I already knew at the beginning, you wouldn't have had time to fall for me."

"But I scheduled a goodbye open house."

Hayes shrugs. "Yeah, that didn't convince me. I knew when it came down to it, you wouldn't sell. You wear your heart on your sleeve, Evie. That's one of my favorite things about you. I knew how much this place meant to you and how much you love the people who come into the shop."

I think of all of the love that the community showed me last night. "Yeah, I do adore everyone in this town."

"They adore you, too. I don't think there was a dry eye in this place when Sweetie recognized you last night," Hayes says thoughtfully.

I think back to those emotional seconds, probably my last with her as herself. It's bittersweet because it was truly amazing to have her back even for that short amount of time but heartbreaking at the same time because I know it will never happen again.

I pull in a breath. "I think that was her goodbye to me. It's weird, and I don't know how to explain it, but I feel deep within my soul that she won't remember me again. It's like she fought through the shroud of confusion with everything she had just to give me those words."

It was her parting gift. And I guess as far as gifts go, it's priceless.

Chapter Twenty-Six

The Christmas tree sparkles with the joy only a Christmas tree can bring. Hayes and I went with a flocked tree this year, so it looks as if it's been kissed by snow. The ribbons and ornaments decorating the tree are pink, white, and silver. It's honestly the most beautiful tree I've ever seen, and perfect for our first Christmas together.

Sweetie would've loved it. She adored pink. And though she left the earth three months ago, I know that wherever she and Pops are in Heaven, they approve.

The past six months have been full of bittersweet moments, as I suppose life often is. Losing Sweetie will always hurt, and I'll always miss her presence, yet I feel her with me all of the time, both her and Pops. I know they're watching over us. My beloved angels.

Hayes has been able to experience a half year of

Cherry Blossom Grove shenanigans. He made it through the entirety of cherry-picking season with the festivals and parades. He now knows what fair week and the color leaf festivals are like. December brings a snow-covered ground along with the skiers that are arriving in our quaint town.

The holidays are beautiful here. Every tree on Main Street is decorated with lights. Each shop window is decked out in more lights and Christmas spirit. Soon, we'll have the holiday light parade, which is always a hit. Santa and his reindeer close the show on the last float and always draw a crowd.

Our days are filled with happiness and laughter. Hayes is still doing consulting work with his firm but no more travel. Some days we work together down in the shop, and other days our employees do. My photography business has really taken off, and I love to see the joy of other people through the lens. Capturing snapshots of perfect little moments in people's lives is so rewarding. We make time to see our friends and participate in community activities that aren't directly linked to the shop. Overall, life is pretty great.

"Are you ready?" Hayes comes out of the bedroom and pulls me from my thoughts.

"Yeah, just admiring the tree."

"It is a pretty one," he says.

"Still no hints about today?"

He shakes his head. "Absolutely not. I told you. It's

an early Christmas present and by extension...a surprise."

"I hate surprises."

"No, you don't"

"You're right. I don't." I chuckle. I love Hayes's surprises. "Do I need to bring anything special?"

"Just yourself." He extends his hand.

I quickly put on my winter coat and thread my fingers through his as he leads us out of the apartment.

"How far is the drive?" I ask.

"Not far."

I'm thankful to have Hayes drive on the snowy roads for me. I've never liked it, but he loves to drive in the snow for some odd reason.

He pulls into the parking lot of the town's high school. There are three large buses parked across the parking lot. The buses are painted purple, and in large colorful letters across each one, it says, *The Love Train* with paintings of cats and dogs.

"The love train?" I question.

"Is multiple shelters that come together and travel around Michigan to try to find animals homes," Hayes replies.

"You're getting me a pet?" I shriek.

Hayes chuckles. "I was thinking about a dog or puppy if you wanted."

I bounce in my seat. "Yes! Oh, my gosh! Thank you. I've always wanted to be a dog person!"

"Well, you have three buses full to choose from."

I bite my lip. "Oh, that's going to be hard to choose. You know I'm going to want to take them all home."

"Yeah, but I think it's probably best to start with one." Hayes turns off the engine. "You ready?"

"Definitely!"

The first bus is filled with mainly cats, a couple of bunnies, and a duck. They're all adorable, but we move on to the second bus to see the dogs. The second bus is for the puppies. Hayes and I hold so many of them, and they're the cutest things in the universe. Puppies are definitely a gift from heaven. Their smell, kisses, little grunts, and puppy breath is incredible.

"I love them all," I tell Hayes as I sit on the ground, a pile of puppies clamoring to climb up my chest. "This is the best day ever."

"Puppies are pretty cute." Hayes smiles, holding a wrinkly little spotted one.

I take a little gray pittie in my hands and hold her to my face. I kiss her cheeks, and she licks me back. She's so beautiful and is going to grow up to be a stunning looking dog.

"Do you want to see the third bus before you decide?" Hayes asks.

I sigh. "I guess, though, that's just going to make it harder." I chuckle. "Seriously, how many can we get?"

Hayes laughs. "Let's start with one, babe. We can work up to more, but we do live in an apartment. Don't you want to see how walking one multiple times a day and picking up poop feels? One may be enough."

"You're right," I groan. "Why do you have to be so levelheaded?" I tease.

The third bus is full of mainly adult dogs, and as soon as I see them, I know I'm not getting a puppy. As much as I love the puppies, so will everyone else. My heart breaks when I think about how long some of these dogs have been living in the shelters. I'm drawn to a long-eared, short thing with graying fur and a foggy eye.

"Can you tell me about this one?" I ask one of the workers.

"Yes, she is a basset hound mix. You can see she got the basset hound ears," the employee says. "We think she's about five years old even though she's graying. But bassets can live to twelve years or more, so she still has a lot of life in her. She is blind in her one eye."

"How long has she been in the shelter?" I ask.

"Almost four years. If I remember correctly, her original owner passed away."

"Can I see her?" I ask, sitting on the ground.

"Sure." The shelter employee opens up the crate, and the short little dog comes strolling out and right into my lap.

I hug her against me and start to cry. I'm not even sure why, but the tears come as I hold this sweet girl against me. It's love at first sight. "It's her. I love her." I stare up to Hayes, who has tears in his eyes.

"I knew you would," he says. "She has a locket on her collar. Open it."

Confused, I feel along her collar to find a silver locket. Hayes is kneeling beside me now. "Open it up."

My eyes dart from the dog's collar to Hayes. I pry the locket open, and a diamond ring falls into my hand. I gasp.

"What's happening right now?"

Hayes takes the ring from my grasp, and on one knee, he holds it out to me. "Evie Emberton, you are the most amazing person I've ever met. I think I fell in love with you almost immediately and concocted this plan where I could stay with you and work beside you, knowing it would become more. You fascinated me from the start. Your love for others, your heart, your wit, and your zest for life is something I don't ever want to live without. The past six months have been the best six months of my life. I love you more than you will ever know. Will you do the honor of becoming my wife?"

I move around the dog as to not scare her, and then I throw myself into Hayes's arms. "Oh my gosh, yes!" I say through tears. "Yes! Yes! Yes! I love you so much, Hayes!"

We kiss and hug, and he places the ring on my finger. "I can't believe this." I look at the beautiful ring on my finger. "But wait...I'm so confused. Why was the ring on her collar?"

"Well, I knew I wanted to do this, so I came here earlier and looked at all of the dogs, and when I saw her,

I knew you'd fall in love with her as soon as you saw her. So I arranged it with the workers so they wouldn't show or sell her to anyone else until I got back with you."

"That was risky."

"I know you, Evie, and I knew which one you'd choose."

"She is pretty perfect, isn't she?" I reach out to the side and pet her soft ears.

"She is," Hayes agrees.

"What should we name her?"

"That's your call."

I look at our new dog. "Cherry," I say.

"It's perfect." Hayes nods. "Very fitting. Cherries have been at the center of everything these past months."

"And living here, they always will," I remind him with a chuckle.

"Yeah, I love it."

"Come here, Cherry," I say to our new family member. She waddles back into my arms, and it's right where she should be.

Hayes fills out the paperwork and buys her a new collar and leash while I hold her in my lap and wrap my hand around her floppy ears. Every few moments, I hold out my hand and look at my ring, and then back at Cherry. Today has certainly been a perfect day.

Cherry does incredible in the car and starts to wag her tail like she knows she's found her people.

Once we're home, she sniffs around the apartment and doesn't bother Pumpkin, who evil eyes her from the couch. He doesn't run off though, so I have hope they'll be buddies soon enough.

"I'm going to run out and get her some food, new dog bowls, a bed, and toys. I wanted to get them prior, but I didn't want to risk ruining the surprise, so I waited." Hayes pulls me into a hug.

"Oh, that's fine. I'll just be here snuggling her while you're gone." I stand on my tiptoes and give him a kiss. "Drive safe."

"Will do. See you soon. I love you."

"I love you," I tell my fiancé.

When I come back into the living room, Cherry is asleep on one side of the couch, and Pumpkin is asleep on the other, and I love it.

I look to the side to see the licorice candy wilted and bending over the sides of the Mason jar in the china cabinet. The licorice sticks have been hardened by six months of exposure now. The purple satin ribbon hangs over the shelf of the china cabinet, where the bouquet holds a treasured place in our home. The short piece of candy is still among the rest, a wish that wasn't pulled.

The night I was given this pile of licorice sticks changed everything. It came to me after making a huge decision to keep Sweet as Pie forever. It brought Hayes back me. It sparked a recognition within Sweetie that gave me a final goodbye and allowed her to hear my parting words of love. The entire bouquet ignited a lifetime of wishes to come true. Today is no exception.

Hayes is my forever, and we share a love like my

parents and grandparents had. I wake up every day grateful for this life.

I didn't need that one licorice wish because each day is already a gift.

It's hard to pick one wish when so many have already been granted.

Dear Readers,

Thank you so much for reading! I hope you loved stepping into the world of Cherry Blossom Grove. While fictional, I modeled Cherry Blossom Grove after my hometown of Chelsea, Michigan. From the adorable shops, old brick buildings that line Main Street, and all the parades—living in small town USA is a pretty great experience.

If you are a veteran Ellie Wade reader, thank you for coming along on this *sweet* side of romance. If you're a new-to-me reader, know that my other romance books have some spice. So, if that's not your cup of tea, stick around for book two in *The Cherry Blossom Grove Series* entitled, *Cherry Kisses*. Coming soon.

I also write cozy mysteries with furry sidekicks under the pen name, Lily Rose Lane.

In addition, I write young adult post-apocalyptic zombie fiction under the pen name, A.R. Howard.

A little random? Yes! But, lots of fun. I just love telling stories that touch people's hearts regardless of the genre.

For all the latest sweet romance Ellie Wade information make sure to sign up for my newsletter, here.

I'm so excited for this series, and I can't wait to share it with you.

You can connect with me on several places, and I would love to hear from you.

Join my readers group: www.facebook.com/groups/wadeswarriorsforthehea

Find me on Facebook: www.facebook.com/ EllieWadeAuthor

Find me on Instagram: www.instagram.com/ authorelliewade

Find me on TikTok: https://www.tiktok.com/@ authorelliewade

Visit my website: www.elliewade.com

Remember, the greatest gift you can give an author is a review. If you feel so inclined, please leave a review on the various retailer sites. It doesn't have to be fancy. A couple of sentences would be awesome!

Thank you again for reading! I am blessed in so many ways, and I am beyond grateful for this beautiful life. XOXO

Forever,

Ellie <3

About the Author

Ellie Wade lives in Michigan with her husband, and three children. She loves all creatures, and, much to her husband's dismay, brings strays home often. She's the loving owner of three dogs, two cats, two bunnies, and chickens. Ellie loves the beauty of her home state, especially the lakes and the gorgeous autumn weather. When she is not writing, you will find her reading, hanging out with her kids, or spending time with family and friends. She loves traveling and exploring new places with her family.

Made in United States
Cleveland, OH
30 June 2025

18167197R00136